THE WORLD ACCORDING TO JENNY

"My sister Chloris, who is two years older, knows more about me than I do and can read my mind. Maybe she can do that because she's older or because she's a Scorpio. Scorpios have strange powers . . . Chloris has this thing about putting labels on people. She had a phase where she called anybody she didn't like a creep. Then at another stage, she called them freaks. As far as I was concerned, I couldn't tell one from the other. The creeps weren't any creepier than the other people, and the freaks weren't any freakier. But you have to remember, Chloris and I are completely different, and we don't see things the same way."

Bantam Books by Kin Platt

CHLORIS AND THE FREAKS
CHLORIS AND THE WEIRDOS

CHLORIS AND THE WEIRDOS

Kin Platt

BANTAM BOOKS · TORONTO · NEW YORK · LONDON

This low-priced Bantam Book
has been completely reset in a type face
designed for easy reading, and was printed
from new plates. It contains the complete
text of the original hard-cover edition.
NOT ONE WORD HAS BEEN OMITTED.

CHLORIS AND THE WEIRDOS

A Bantam Book | published by arrangement with
Bradbury Press, Inc.

PRINTING HISTORY

Bradbury Press edition published November 1978
2nd printing .... October 1979
Bantam edition | May 1980

ISBN 0–553–13315–2

Published simultaneously in the United States and Canada

PRINTED IN THE UNITED STATES OF AMERICA

0 9 8 7 6 5 4 3 2 1

To Audrey Kenevan

CHLORIS
AND THE
WEIRDOS

1

I never thought I would be in love by age thirteen. I can't believe it. It's one of the totally most unexpected things to ever happen to me.

His name is Harold Osborne. His nickname is Hawk. He calls himself H²O. I feel silly calling him Hawk, and I don't care for the name Harold. Calling him the sign for water is even worse. It's really far out that when I finally do get my first boyfriend, he would have three names, and I don't like any of them.

But far out describes Harold the Hawk Osborne. He has an interesting and wild sense of humor, and happens to be a dedicated skateboarder. He does all the tricks. The flip-kicks. End-overs. Nose releases. Space dogs. You have to be a "scootie" to know what the rest are called. It's all under the heading of spinning their slicks. There are a lot of skateboarders scooting around. They seem to be all over the place. Tilting. Careening. Tripping and falling.

Like me, Harold the Hawk Osborne goes to Emerson Junior High. But I don't get to see much of him because half the time he's covered with bandages from bad falls. Like some of the other dedicated skateboarders around, Harold the Hawk likes to ride empty swimming pools. He goes up and down, around the sides, riding the pool rim, doing what he calls tail-tappers and frontal one-wheelers. They call it carving. Falling off is called space walking.

The skateboard, Harold the Hawk says, is possi-

bly his very best friend. Whenever he feels down at
school, he can always go home and take his best
friend out of the closet, he says.

He dresses normally at school. But at the skateboard competitions, he wears all that jazz. Adidas
shoes, shorts, elbow and knee pads, helmet. Cycle
gloves. They need that stuff for protection.

My sister Chloris, who is two years older, knows
more about me than I do and can read my mind.
Maybe she can do that because she's older or because
she's a Scorpio. Scorpios have strange powers. Chloris
was the one who told me I was in love with Harold
the Hawk.

"And just your luck," she said, "you had to fall for
a weirdo."

Chloris has this thing about putting labels on
people. She had a phase where she called anybody
she didn't like a creep. Then at another stage, she
called them freaks. As far as I was concerned, I
couldn't tell one from the other. The creeps weren't
any creepier than the other people, and the freaks
weren't any freakier. But you have to remember,
Chloris and I are completely different, and we don't
see things the same way.

I fell into the trap just as I had all the other
times. "What makes him a weirdo?"

"I've seen that boy. He lives on his skateboard."

"So what? All skateboarders do."

"If you get married, he'll meet you at the church
on his skateboard," Chloris said. "He'll go down the
aisle on his skateboard. When you go on your honeymoon, you'll have to make him take his board off
before he goes to bed."

I could see she might have a point there. "Well,
anyway, he's only fourteen. Who said anything about
getting married?"

"I just thought I'd warn you in advance, Jenny.
You have to be real careful about hanging out with

weirdos. They can wear out your mind if you let them."

"How can they do that?"

She shrugged. "That's how weirdos operate. It just comes natural to them."

This day we were having another sister-to-sister conversation in our bedroom after school. Mom was still at work, doing her number for Bontel's store in the cosmetics and perfume department. Stuff for skin, hair and nails. Junk like powder, lipstick and those gooey face creams. Those are the cosmetics. The perfumes are what I like. Those neat flowery smells. We were out of fathers for the time being, and it was just Mom, Chloris and me to make up our happy family.

Chloris can be funny or she can be a pain. There are no halfway measures with her. She's either up or she's down. She likes people or she doesn't. She doesn't hold her feelings back and gets it all out of her system. Either everybody shapes up the way she wants her world to be, or Chloris won't play.

Scorpios can be that extreme. They're the hubs of the world. The doers, the movers. They make the wheels move, make things happen.

I'm a Libra, and we Librans like to balance things, think them over. What that amounts to is that I'm just another wheel for my sister Chloris to move around. It doesn't mean that I'm her slave exactly. She simply has more drive inside herself to dominate. And I really couldn't care less about who wins.

I mean as long as everything is peaceful and comes out all right.

I would have liked Harold the Hawk to be a Libra like me. That would have made him better balanced, and then maybe he wouldn't fall off his skateboard so much. But he's a Gemini, the third sign of the zodiac. The sign of the Heavenly Twins. Natives of this sign are usually quick-witted and very bright. Librans and Gemini people are harmonious, and that's probably why Harold the Hawk and I get along.

He doesn't agree. He doesn't think all that much about astrology. He thinks it's because we're both getting "radical." Getting radical, in skateboarding jargon, means "letting loose," trying to get as aggressive as possible.

The idea that anybody would ever consider me aggressive was very surprising to me. I always thought I was more the shy, retiring type.

Harold the Hawk explained it to me. "You're a jogger. I'm a skateboarder. We do our things by ourselves. We're not dependent on anyone."

"Aggressive?" I said. "Me?"

He nodded firmly. "That's how we met. You were running down the street, and you wouldn't give up your space for me coming the other way on my board. That's why I took that big fall, and that's what makes you aggressive."

"I was there first," I said. "You came around the corner."

"You could have stepped off into the grass, and kept on jogging," he said. "I ran out of sidewalk."

"Well, you keep telling me you ride the board all the time because you need the practice. You might as well practice falling," I said.

"You don't get points for falling. What are you doing Friday night?"

Nobody had ever asked me that before. "My homework. Why?"

Harold the Hawk was spinning on his board, making the nose go up and around. I've heard of but never seen something called a whirling dervish. I suppose Harold the Hawk looked like one then. "I thought maybe we could go to a movie."

Nobody had ever asked me to go to a movie before, either. Except my Mom, or Chloris. "I'll have to ask my mother," I told him. "What's playing?"

"*Star Wars.*"

"Okay," I said. "But you might as well know right now, I'm a virgin."

Harold the Hawk did a flip-kick and lost his best friend. "That's okay. So am I."

"Well, then, call me tonight," I said.

"I don't know your number."

"It's in the book," I said.

2

It was a year since Mom divorced Fidel, and I was slowly climbing out of my depression. For a long, long time, I was in a terrible rut, feeling sorry for Fidel, feeling sorry for myself. I missed Fidel's big house and studio in Tiger Tail Canyon, and the talking morning birds, and I missed my best friend Kathy Kingman, who lived just up the canyon from us.

Kathy was twelve then, like me, and her mother Mrs. Kingman was telling Kathy's father to get lost and not come back, about the same time. We both were a couple of sad sacks. My Mom's divorce came first, making her a two-time loser, but we left Fidel's house before it became final. Then it was up to the lawyers and the court, about a six months' deal. Leaving Fidel really wrecked me, drove me right up the wall, and I had to keep telling myself a hundred times a day that it's over, it's over—so it must be over. And gradually the bad feelings went away.

When Kathy's mother got her divorce, her first one, they stayed on in the house Mr. Kingman got for them. We moved back to an apartment in Westwood and I hated it after the peaceful country feeling of Tiger Tail Canyon.

Kathy's mom was a lot younger than mine, about ten years, really terrific looking, a former Miss Texas beauty queen, and she started to date right away. Kathy's father moved out to a job with computers in Texas.

Our Mom cooled it and only dated one guy she met on her job. This was Duane Turner. Chloris called him a freak and for once I agreed with my sister about something. But I had to admit it was mostly because I loved Fidel La Mancha so, and this new guy Duane was a lot younger and dressed and acted too slick. So I hated him on sight when it looked as if he was going to move right in and be our third father.

But Chloris turned against Duane Turner, hating him just as she had Fidel and all the other guys Mom dated before him. She was being loyal to our original daddy, she thought, who had dumped on himself with a gun and committed suicide. Chloris claimed he loved her and was still talking to her long after he died, until Mom took her to Dr. Smythe, the lady shrink in Beverly Hills, who charged an arm and a leg just for people sitting down and telling her their thoughts.

After Mom unloaded Fidel, Chloris got better fast and stopped yakking to me about what a great daddy our daddy was. I don't remember him because I was so young. What she wanted was Fidel out of the way, and then Duane, no new daddy at all for us. Mom couldn't take Chloris calling her new guy Duane a freak, finally ditched him, and Chloris got her way.

That's the story about us Carpenters, so far. I don't blame or hate anybody. I was just hanging in there waiting for something nice to happen, and it finally did with my meeting Harold the Hawk.

Chloris was going to Uni High School, and working part-time as a waitress at Patsy's Pizza Parlor. She put in about three to five hours, and was making about ten dollars a night with tips. And she was socking it all away for her new car when she went to college. Before, when Mom gave her allowance, she was pretty generous with her money, but as soon as she started making her own, she really became a miser and wouldn't spend a dime on anything.

I was still considered too young to get a job, except for some occasional baby-sitting nights Chloris passed over to me. The Keltons and the Logans and Dr. and Mrs. Klugherz, they were my steadiest customers.

But the trouble was, baby-sitting came at night, and with both Chloris and my mom working late, I was the only one with any free time. So guess who had the job of preparing dinner?

When I get a real steady job like Chloris, I'm not going to be cheap like she is. The first thing I'm going to do with my money is hire a cook. The way it is now, the only thing I'm any good at is making tacos, and even though I'm crazy about them, there comes a point where neither I nor anybody else in the family can look at a taco face to face.

I discussed this problem with Harold the Hawk, and was surprised to learn that he did a lot of the cooking for his mother who works. Harold the Hawk is also a victim of divorce, as they say about our generation.

"I make pretty good fried chicken," he said. "It's no big deal. You just heat up some oil and drop some chicken parts in. You turn them over when the kitchen starts smoking, and when you have to open the window wider, they're all done."

I told him that was a thought.

"Lamb chops are easy," he said. "You just put them on the broiler and when you hear everything snapping and popping inside there, you know they're ready."

"I was going to hire a cook when I started working. Maybe I'll hire you."

"I do a terrific baloney omelet, too," Harold said. "You just heat up a couple of slices of the baloney. Then you beat on some eggs. Then you pour the eggs on, and when it starts burning, you turn it over, and it's all done."

"Do you do all this on your skateboard?" I asked.

"Well, for a while I did, but the wheels make marks on the linoleum, my mom raised heck, and then I got to scrub the whole kitchen floor down. I know what you're doing. You're trying to make me feel guilty for having so much fun on my board. Don't forget, it beats surfing. You don't have to wait for a wave."

I could picture Harold the Hawk preparing dinner for his mom on his skateboard, nearly burning the place down, and I had to laugh. Maybe Chloris is right, and I really am in love. I think love is being able to laugh at somebody you like.

3

I told Mom about *Stars Wars* and Harold the Hawk and she wanted to know what that was all about. Chloris was just leaving for her job as Miss Universe at Patsy's Pizza place.

"He's a weirdo," Chloris said.

"He is not," I said.

Mom frowned and pushed back her hair. "You're

always characterizing people, putting tags on them. What makes him a weirdo?"

Chloris shrugged. She and Mom had a longtime feud going. "Well, you know what a weirdo is, don't you?"

Mom looked cross. "Maybe I do. But I'd like to hear your idea of one."

"He's always on his skateboard," Chloris said. "He'll probably pick Jenny up on his skateboard for the movie."

Mom looked at me. Knowing what little I did about Harold the Hawk, I didn't want to bet Chloris was wrong. "I don't think he's that dumb," I said. "If he is, I won't go. Anyway, we have to get a bus to the movie, and besides, Mom hasn't said if I can go yet."

Mom toyed with her hair. "I don't know." She turned to Chloris. "I see a lot of young people on skateboards. He's probably a nice boy. Why do you call him weirdo?"

Chloris hesitated. I could read her mind this time. She didn't want to go on about it and ruin my first chance for a date. "Well, maybe he isn't exactly a weirdo."

I sighed, relieved, but Chloris couldn't let it rest. "Maybe he's a frock. That's kind of in between a freak and a jock."

Mom shook her head. "You'll be late for work," she said pointedly. "Let's hope you don't get any weirdos tonight to wait on. They might spoil your whole evening."

Chloris grinned. "Besides weirdos, freaks, and frocks, jocks and brains, creeps and crumbs, there are also potheads, pinheads, and idiots."

"Which one are you?" I said, but Chloris was already going out the door.

"If you ask me," Mom said, "your sister isn't entirely normal herself."

"She's just trying to be funny," I said.

Mom sniffed. "Maybe."

"So can I go with Harold the Hawk?"

"Is that his name?"

"Well, sort of a nickname."

"That's odd," Mom said.

"You mean weird?"

"No," Mom said firmly. "Simply odd. An odd name."

4

Chloris got home that night a little later than usual. Mom was taking a bath. It was nearly eleven o'clock but for some reason I wasn't too sleepy. Maybe it was the excitement about my first date.

"What took you so long?" I said. "Did they promote you to dishwasher?"

Chloris slammed her bag down. I hadn't realized she was angry. "That's the last time I'm ever going to fall for that," she said.

"Fall for what?"

"Some guy offered to drive me home."

"Who was it?"

"Some weirdo." She went over to the dresser and looked at herself in the mirror. "What did Mom say?"

"She hasn't made up her mind yet. What happened with your weirdo?"

Chloris was brushing her hair. "He didn't want to let me out of his car until I kissed him good night."

I wondered if I was going to have that same

problem with Harold the Hawk. A bus is nearly as bad as a car. And if you don't make up your mind, you can miss your stop. "Was he good looking?" I said.

Chloris looked pityingly at me. "Well, you don't think I would have let him drive me home if he wasn't, do you?"

"Yeah, but you also said he was a weirdo, remember?"

Chloris grimaced. "Well, I didn't know that then. Up till then, he was just the order of pizza with pepperoni. He has it every night."

"How old is he?"

"Eighteen, at least he says he is. He's a senior at school."

"Was it his own car?"

Chloris shrugged. "How would I know? Do you think I would ask this weirdo if this was his own car?"

I had a sudden wish that Harold the Hawk would grow out of his skateboard fast and into a car of his own. "So in other words, he wasn't such a hot date, this weirdo."

Chloris was examining her lips closely with the hand mirror. "It wasn't a date, Jenny. How would I know how he is on a date? This was just a simple ride home. I didn't feel like standing and waiting for the bus, that's all, and when Wayne offered me this ride—"

"Wayne who?"

"Wayne Gavin. He's part French, I think. Part French, part pepperoni pizza and part weirdo."

"Was he a good kisser?"

Chloris made a wry face. "Ugh. Echh. Like that."

"So why did you do it?"

"Well, I had to get out of the car, didn't I? If I didn't kiss him, I might have to spend the whole night out there with that weirdo." She looked around suddenly. "Don't tell Mom. She doesn't want me to take any rides."

"Okay. When's your next date with this Wayne Gavin?"

Chloris fell down on my bed. "Never, I hope. I wish he would go somewhere else for his pizza. I don't need his free rides home. Especially if there's a catch to them."

"I still don't see what makes him a weirdo," I said. "A lot of people eat pizza with pepperoni. You told me that weirdos wear out your mind. How did he do that?"

"Well, I told you, didn't I? He wouldn't let me out of his car if I didn't kiss him good night."

"You mean he locked the door on your side?"

Chloris sniffed. "Something like that."

"But all you have to do is lift the handle and it unlocks."

Chloris nodded, looking at her feet. "Well, that's what I mean about how they can wear out your mind. I mean I didn't even think of that."

"I bet," I said.

"Anyway," Chloris said, "it's no big deal. Kissing a boy is no big deal. It doesn't mean a thing. Especially if he happens to be a weirdo."

I was about to ask her what the difference was when Mom came out of the bathroom. She looked at my desk.

"Have you finished your homework?"

"All done," I said.

She looked at Chloris. "How about yours?"

"I just got home."

Mom nodded. "You're working to make money so you can get your own car. We're not living on your earnings. You still have to do your homework. Either that or give up your job."

Chloris' temper flared. "I didn't say I wasn't going to do it. I said I just got home."

"Well, you'll never do it lying there," Mom said.

She walked out and headed for the living room, and the TV.

"That's what I get for going out with a weirdo," Choris said. "He cost me a good fifteen minutes of homework time."

5

The next morning, before going to work, Mom told me it was okay for me to see *Star Wars* with Harold.

"Harold the Hawk," I said.

Mom wrinkled her nose. "I don't like that name."

"Neither do I."

Mom looked at me as if wondering who was crazy. "Just be sure you come right home after the movie. I'm sure your sister can give you a lot of pointers on that."

There's always that kind of battle going on between them, and I've learned to live with it without taking sides. "We'll probaby make the early show," I said. "And be right back, unless Harold the Hawk decides to treat me to some ice cream or something."

"Ice cream doesn't take all night," Mom said. "I still expect you home by eleven."

"No sweat, Mom. Solid," I said.

She looked at me. "Why do you talk that way?"

I shrugged. "I guess all the kids do, Mom."

"That's no excuse," she said, kissing me good-bye.

Chloris was hogging the bathroom, doing her face. "Don't make it look too good," I said. "You'll only attract more weirdos."

"What did Mom say?" she asked.

"She said it was okay, I could go, only I have to be home by eleven."

"Rotsa ruck," she said. "I bet your skateboard weirdo can't even tell time."

"He's not a weirdo," I said. "You've got weirdos on the brain."

"You think so? Wait till you see what Mom brings home next. I can hardly wait."

Suddenly I had an insight into what Chloris was doing. All the talk about weirdos that didn't seem to make sense. She was waiting for Mom to have another boyfriend, determined that she wouldn't let Mom bring home another possible husband and father for us. She was still holding on to her childhood memory of our daddy who had killed himself after Mom divorced him.

She couldn't wait now for Mom to bring home another guy so she could call him a weirdo.

"She said she wouldn't get married again until we grew up. Remember?"

Chloris shook her head, biting her lip and smiling into the bathroom mirror. "No way. She's getting too old to wait. She'll have to do it soon. As soon as she finds the right weirdo."

"I don't care," I said. "I miss Fidel, but it's okay now. I don't care if she wants another husband."

Chloris put down her lipstick and stared at me. "That's the trouble with you, Jenny. You don't have any character. If you had any character, you wouldn't want another father. You'd stick up for your rights."

"I don't care," I said. "I'm tired of sticking up for them. If it will make her happy, I don't care."

Chloris nodded. "That's what I mean about not

having any character. And don't come crying to me
when she brings home her new weirdo."

"Maybe he'll be nice. Fidel was."

Chloris gave me her withering look. She stalked
out without another word.

I shouted after her. "Well, he was! You just
didn't appreciate him. He was nice to us both. You
just never gave him a chance."

Before I knew it I was crying. A whole year had
passed and I thought I had gotten completely over
Fidel, and would never cry over that again. I guess
Chloris was right, and I didn't have any character.

6

I wondered how Harold the Hawk would act on
our first date out. Boys were supposed to be very
headstrong, I had heard. They liked to dominate, be
in charge, and have their own way. I really knew
awfully little about boys.

Ordinarily I might not have given it a second
thought, just spent my time idly dreaming, feeling a
nice soft and warm glow about me and Harold. A first
date can be awfully exciting. It made me feel very
gentle inside and romantic. But there were the Wom-
en's Lib people now, and they were making a lot of
flak about how things used to be and they were fed
up and not going to take it anymore. The women's
rights thing.

The idea is that girls are supposed to be recognized for what we are, not allow ourselves to be regarded as love objects to be pushed around and manipulated. In other words I had to be careful and suspicious of boys. I didn't like that idea at all. This was my first time to be a love object for anybody, and I wanted to be able to make up my own mind about whether I was being pushed around or manipulated. These new rules seemed kind of silly and I wished these Women's Libbers had waited a little longer before deciding this was the way it had to be.

But it made me tense and wary, and I was uptight about it the following day when Harold the Hawk caught up to me at school. Apparently he had been waiting for me so that we could talk before going to class, leaning against the wall watching the kids go by. He was on foot, not wearing his best friend. He had sneakers on, yellow cord pants, a checked blue shirt which went okay with his flaming red hair.

"Hey, how we doing about Friday night?" he said as I came up. "Did you ask your mom about it, if it was okay?"

Well, I thought, that's just a question, he's not dominating. "She said it was okay." But I was still uptight, so I added needlessly, "How about *your* mom?"

He didn't take notice of my sarcasm. "Well, she made it kind of heavy. She wanted to know who you are, why I want to take you out to a movie, and so on. Stuff like that. I said you were okay."

All my Libran instincts went up in the air. "How do you know I'm okay? I don't have wheels like your board."

Harold the Hawk waved his hands and forgot he was holding books. They went down and he stooped after them. It was a good chance to kick him, and I probably wouldn't get a better one, but my good nature held me back somehow.

"If I wanted to take my board to a movie, I wouldn't have asked you, Jen. What you don't understand is, I'm her only child, and she doesn't want anything to happen to me."

My voice went up along with my temper. "Like what could happen? It's only a movie, right?"

"Right."

I looked at him. He looked uncomfortable and honest.

"Well, then," I said.

"She's probably worried that I might fall in love or something, and she would lose a good cook."

"From what you told me, Harold, you're not such a hot cook. You burn everything."

He nodded. His face was nearly as red as his hair, which is saying a lot. "That's quite true. But my mom doesn't like to make judgments about my cooking. So she doesn't come off the wall about it. The most she'll say is, 'Well, next time it will be better.'"

I noticed that Harold the Hawk was acting like a true Gemini native. Keeping an open mind. Anxious to learn new things. It reminded me that I'd better get myself back to being an evenly balanced Libran.

"She sounds easygoing. What does she work at?"

"She's a policewoman."

I never expected that. "You mean with a gun and everything?"

Harold shrugged. "It's a new world, Jen. A lot of women nowadays are proving they're just as good as men, if not better at their jobs."

I stared hard. He looked and sounded serious.

"Well, okay," I said. "There's just one thing, though. I have to be home by eleven."

"No sweat," he said. "Me, too."

I let that go. "And no skateboards, right? It'll be just you and me and the bus to the movie in Westwood."

"Well, sure. Is seven o'clock okay?"

"Seven? I guess so."

"Thanks," he said. "You got it."

Then he waved his hand and went off without trying to push me around or manipulate me any longer.

7

Chloris was already home when I got back from school. She was on the phone, and she pulled it closer to her when she saw me. "Well, maybe I will and maybe I won't," she said into the phone. "I can't guarantee anything." She lay back on her twin bed, her knees up, jabbing her finger at the phone while she listened.

"That your pepperoni-pizza freak?" I said and she nodded.

She listened for a while, rolling her eyes. "Yeah, I know. You can't breathe without me, right?"

I was going to take my books and myself out of the room so she could talk, but she held up her hand to stop me. She smiled into the phone. "Well, of course, I'll be there tonight. It's my job, isn't it? If you're at my table, I'll wait on you. I think I know your order by heart already. Let me think. Pizza pepperoni, right?" She listened, and laughed. "All right. Maybe I'll see you around, then."

She dropped the phone on its cradle and offered it to me to put back on the night table. I pretended not to see it. She got up grunting and put it between our beds. "Thanks a lot," she said.

I ignored that. "How come he's calling you? Did you give him your phone number?"

Chloris sniffed and pushed back her hair. "Do you think I'd give my number out to a weirdo like that? Guess again."

"So how did he get it?"

She shrugged, yawning. "How would I know? He knew my name, and I guess he remembered where I live from the time he drove me home. That's not too difficult even for a weirdo."

"What's he trying to do, date you?"

"I suppose he is. But if he thinks I'm going out with him the first time he asks, he's got another think coming."

I remembered not putting up too much of a fight when Harold the Hawk asked me out. "Why's that?"

Chloris sat up, hugging her knees. "Well, you don't want to make it too easy for them, do you? I mean, if you grab at their first offer, they'll think you're desperate, that you don't have anybody else to go out with."

"Well, yeah, but what if you don't?"

Chloris smoothed her blouse front. "They still don't have to know that, do they? You never want to give a boy an advantage like that."

I sat down opposite her, trying to learn some of these things about boys. "Why not?"

"Because if they find you're too easy to date, too eager to please, you lose them fast. They dump on you."

"Gy," I said. It sounds like the word "guy." A lot of kids in L.A. say "gy" for "gee," "gosh," or "golly." I got if from Chloris, and now she's stopped using it. Except to mimic me.

She grinned maliciously at me now, her green eyes gleaming. "Gy-y-y-y. You mean you made a date right away with your skateboard weirdo, right?"

"Well, sort of."

"That's tough. You should have asked me first. That's what an older sister is for, isn't it?"

I was surprised to hear Chloris thinking that way. "Yeah, I guess. Only if I'd listened to you, I would have said no, and then I wouldn't have a date for Friday."

She sniffed. "Big deal. You're only going to a movie, right. What's such a big deal about a movie?"

I couldn't think of an answer to that. All I knew was that inside of me, it was a very big deal. Maybe it was first-date fever, or whatever. Anyway, I couldn't see myself playing Chloris' kind of game, making believe you have a date when you don't.

"How many times is he supposed to ask before you do date him?" I said.

She pursed her lips and looked at her fingernails. "It all depends," she said. "Sometimes you can play too hard to get, and they wind up with somebody else. So you have to play it by ear, Jen, you know."

"Yeah, well, that sounds dumb to me. If you like somebody, why can't you say so and go out with him?"

Chloris got up and stretched. "Nobody is saying that you can't, dumbbell. All I'm saying is you don't want to make it too easy for them. You heard me just before. You didn't hear me giving in right off, did you?"

"No, but you keep saying he's a weirdo. So maybe that's why you can act so hard to get."

Chloris smiled. "You think so? Wait till you see him. All the other kids fall all over him."

"So then why—?"

Chloris flipped her hand. "It's part of the same thing, dummy. You can't act too eager whether they're really weird or not, see?"

I frowned, shook my head. "No, I don't."

She was walking out of the room. "You will. You'll get it some day. Rotsa ruck meanwhile."

The phone rang and she turned and dashed toward it. "Carpenter residence," she said in her TV commercial voice. The look of anticipation left her face, replaced by a frown. "Hold on." She handed me the phone. "It's your weirdo—wants to talk to you."

I grabbed the phone. "Hello?"

"Hi," he said. "Was that your sister?"

I nodded. "Yeah." I hunched over the phone. Chloris was still standing there. I made hand signals for her to get lost. She tossed her hair and flounced out. "Anything wrong about Friday?" I said nervously.

"I get it," he said. "You want to remind me we have a date. You might as well know right now I'm not the type who cancels."

"Me, neither," I said happily.

"I'm glad to hear that," he said. "Once I make up my mind, that's it."

"Well, me, too, Harold," I said. For some reason, he made every word I said sound sweet and soft.

"I was just wondering if you were going to do any jogging this afternoon."

"Maybe later. I was just about to get into my homework." Then I caught myself up. "Why?" I said.

"I thought maybe I could meet you out there. I've got a few new things to work out on my board before the competition next week."

"What kind of things?"

"Some aerial spinners. Rotations. One-eighties and three-sixties."

"What are those?"

"Oh, you know, spinning around."

I remembered him whirling like a dervish the other time. "You do those pretty good, I thought."

"Oh, a few aren't too difficult. Doing twenty or thirty is the real trick."

"What's the most you've ever done?"

"Six—no, five."

"Oh, well—you'll get it, Harold."

"I've got to get up on my head and hand-stand, too. Is this conversation boring to you?"

"Why, no. Not at all. I just don't know too much about it, that's all."

"There's not that much to it. Once you see an event and hear what everything is called, it's fairly easy. It just takes a certain kind of persistence to get good at it. Not like your sport."

"How's that, Harold?"

"Running takes endurance. And stamina. Once you reach your own wall, you can go through it. With the skateboard, it's going over the same things pretty much, you know. Refining, perfecting things."

"You left out falling, Harold."

"Well, sure. That's another difference, of course. There's a certain risk to the board. But that's what makes it interesting. How long will your homework take?"

"A few hours. I don't know if—"

He whistled. "No, we better forget it. I've got to start dinner in an hour. This is a real big deal I'm making. It takes three hours."

I laughed. "What are you making?"

"Irish stew with dumplings."

"Why does it take so long?"

"Well, actually it only takes two and a half. It's the dumplings that drive me up the wall. They keep coming apart. Dumplings have no character, you know?"

"Do you have a recipe?"

"I have three recipes. I find that if you follow one recipe closely, it never works out. You need to follow two or three to balance things out."

Suddenly I remembered the terrific stews Fidel used to make. He cut the meat up, cut the vegetables up, sprinkled the meat with flour and browned it, then threw everything into a big pot and let it simmer. "You let it simmer gently," Fidel once told me. "The stew had to find its own self."

"I'll give you a female tip on your stew, Harold," I said. "After you sprinkle on the flour, and let it brown, you let the stew simmer gently."

"Hey, is that a fact? No kidding. Maybe if I simmer it gently, the stuff won't burn on me."

"Add enough water, Harold. Or a little wine."

"Wine? Terrific. Anything else?"

I squinted, trying to remember. "You don't add the potatoes until the very end. The last thirty minutes or so."

"Got it," he said. "Hey, I didn't know you were such a terrific cook."

"Well, you never asked me," I said modestly.

"How much flour?"

I saw it in Fidel's big brown hand. "Just a sprinkle. You roll it in flour lightly."

"Anything else?"

"*Bon appetit,* Harold."

I hung up feeling happy and sad. It was nice that Fidel came back into my life this way. It didn't hurt as much.

8

Getting ready for my date Friday night was exciting. I had to do my hair, and then borrow Mom's dryer and sit around forever under it listening to my hair frying. I had to iron my blouse. I was so nervous I nearly burned it. I had to decide which wedgies to put on. I couldn't make up my mind between a skirt and jeans. I didn't want to frighten Harold so I went for the jeans. Still nervous, I borrowed some of Chloris' stuff and did my nails. Then I went all out and sprayed some of Mom's good stuff over me.

Chloris held her nose and waved a newspaper up and down. "You're not supposed to drown yourself in it, dumbbell," she said. "Just a quick whiff of it."

"Well, it comes out too fast," I said.

Chloris kept trying to move the air in the room with the newspaper, pretending she was coughing, fighting for breath. "You'll drive him away with all that stuff on. You and he will be sitting on opposite sides of the movie."

I looked at the time. "Maybe it will wear off by seven. It's only six now."

"Take another shower," Chloris said.

Instead I went out on our little outside patio for a while letting the breeze dilute some of Mom's good Givenchy perfume. I didn't want to waste it all, and after a few seconds, went back inside.

"I can still smell you," Chloris said. *"Yech!"*

"That's tough. It'll wear off in a while."

"Where are you going after the movie?"

"How do I know. This is my first date."

"A lot of kids go to Ship's," Chloris said. "They do a pretty good hamburger, and their chili isn't bad."

"Where did you go your first date?"

"My first date couldn't afford to go anyplace. We came right on home."

"Did you have to kiss him good night?"

Chloris grinned. "I don't have to tell you everything about my personal life."

"I know. Well, did you?"

Chloris yawned. "I don't remember. That was about a hundred dates ago."

"I think it's more like a dozen. You didn't become Miss America until you took the pizza place job."

"That doesn't mean I couldn't have had a hundred, you know. I'm kind of particular whom I go out with. I don't go out with weirdos, for one thing. I've got better things to do with my spare time."

The telephone rang before I could answer her. Chloris yawned. That meant she wasn't expecting a call and I was supposed to answer. I hoped it wasn't Harold the Hawk beginning to get cold feet about our date.

"Hello," I said. "Carpenter residence."

It was Mom. She said she wouldn't be home for dinner because she had to work late.

"Okay, have a good time," I said.

"I said I'm working," Mom said crossly. "Have you and your sister done your homework yet?"

I said I'd done some not all, I didn't know about Chloris. "Well, get to it," she said.

"I'm not exactly in the mood for homework," I said. "Tonight's my date for the movie with Harold the Hawk."

"Oh, I forgot about that," Mom said. "Do you think you'll be eating with your friend after the movie?"

"I don't know. I've got some money in case he's broke."

Mom laughed. "Well, don't spend it all. You'll spoil him for next time."

"With two dollars and thirty-five cents?"

"I'm sure he'll have some money of his own," Mom said. "But just in case, you and your sister can make some hamburgers or open a can of tuna."

"I'm not hungry," I said. "I'm nervous."

"There's nothing to be nervous about. You always wanted to see that movie."

"I know. But I never expected to be seeing it with Harold the Hawk."

"I wish you'd find another name for that boy," Mom said. "I don't know why, but it irritates me."

"Okay. Harold Osborne."

"That sounds better," Mom said. "You'll remember what I said about coming home before eleven?"

"I don't even know if I'm going yet. He hasn't called, and what if he chickens out?"

Mom laughed. "He won't. What time do you expect him?"

"He said seven."

"Then just relax and be ready when he calls. It's been so long, I can't even remember my first date, but I'm sure I felt the same way."

"Okay. What time will you be home?"

"Before you do, I hope. If not, as soon as I can. Be sure the door is locked."

"Okay."

"What are you wearing?"

"My pink blouse and jeans."

"That's fine," Mom said. "Well, have a good time."

"You, too," I said automatically.

"I told you before," Mom said, but then softened her tone. "Good night, Jennifer."

She hung up then and so did I. Chloris had heard me.

"Don't tell me," she said. "She has to work overtime, right? Inventory? I wonder who she's dating this time."

Mom had had to work late several times in the past. Sometimes after that, some new guy would drop around and take her out. Chloris hated them all on sight.

"She's working," I said. "She got mad when I told her to have a good time."

Chloris sniffed. "She'll probably work an extra hour, and then she'll go out to dinner with some new weirdo."

"Well, we haven't met any new guys lately."

"That doesn't mean she isn't dating them," Chloris said. "Nobody is that busy working at Bontel's. She meets somebody, and they ask her out to dinner, and she just tells us she's working overtime. Then before you know it, some new weirdo will be showing up here at the door."

"He might not be a weirdo," I said. "What if he happens to be nice?"

Chloris curled her lip. "No way. You wait and see. Before you know it, you'll have to be saying hello to some new weirdo she found."

There was a sound at the door. I looked at my watch.

"He's early," I said. "It's only a quarter to seven."

"That's what I mean about weirdos," Chloris said. "You never can depend on them."

9

"Hey, I want to thank you," Harold the Hawk said. "The stew came out terrific. My mom liked it so much she left me a big tip." He showed me a bill. "We're loaded tonight."

"I'm glad, Harold. How about the dumplings. How did they come out?"

"Not too bad. A little soggy but at least they weren't all over the place. Next time I'll ask you how you do them."

"All right," I said. I knew dumplings were tough. I would have to study up and practice but it would be worth it.

He had everything figured out. "The bus comes by at seven eleven. It's eighteen minutes to Westwood. Three minutes for the light change, and six to walk to the movie. That makes it seven thirty-eight. The line is only a half block long then and we'll be on time for the eight o'clock showing."

The movie line was slightly longer than he thought and we didn't get inside until five after eight. Harold looked at his watch and shook his head. "There weren't this many people when I checked it on a dry run. Next time I'll make a rough estimate."

"It's okay," I said. "There are plenty of seats. Do you want to sit up front or in the rear?"

"I don't care. How do you feel about the sides or middle?"

"I think the middle. How do you feel about the middle?"

"It's okay. That bus was two minutes late."

He held my arm as we went down the aisle. "Hey, I like the perfume that girl in blue is wearing."

"That's me, not her, Harold," I said.

"Oh. It's a neat smell. Is it your sister's?"

"No, my mom's. Givenchy."

"There are two seats."

"Well, yeah, but a lady is sitting between them. Did I put on too much?"

"No, I didn't notice her. How about over there?"

"That's not the middle, Harold. It's the side."

"I should have made it the six forty-eight bus. There's a better choice of seats. That sure is a neat smell."

"Here's two," I said. "I'm glad you like it."

"You hold them," he said, "I'll get the popcorn."

"I don't feel like popcorn, Harold. I just ate."

"Me, too. Will you be hungry later?"

"I don't know. Ask me later."

He bumped his elbow against mine on the seat

rest. "Hey, is it all right if I put my arm over the back of your seat?"

"I don't know yet. Okay, I guess."

The picture started. I could feel his arm hanging there. I'd heard about boys who start that way. But after a short while, I heard Harold the Hawk moan. "What's wrong?" I said.

"My arm's getting numb. Do you mind if I take it off the back of your seat?"

"No, Harold. That's okay."

"Do you like the movie so far?"

"So far it's just the credits, Harold."

After that, he settled down and we tried to concentrate on the movie. It was very difficult for me because I knew I could almost always see a movie, but this was my very first date with a boy. And so my attention went back and forth between the movie and Harold the Hawk Osborne, who would touch knees with me and then recoil as if my knees had barbed wire on them.

I noticed out of the corner of my eye that he was looking at me a lot, and I spent some time taking quick glimpses of him, and so I suppose neither one of us saw too much of *Star Wars*. But I feel it really was a neat movie, and maybe some day I'll see it again and concentrate more on what's going on up there on the screen.

After it was over, Harold Osborne asked me if I was hungry, and I said I thought I was, sort of, and he said he thought he was, too, sort of.

We were outside now being pushed around by the big crowd breaking out of the place. "I wish I had my skateboard now," Harold said. "I bet I'd scatter a lot of them."

"I bet you would," I said. "There's Ship's across the street, if you still feel hungry."

"Okay," he said. "Let's go."

He took my arm and we were walking across on

the green when I noticed the time. "I promised my mom I'd be home by eleven."

Harold looked at his watch. "There's a ten forty-six bus, which will get you home at five after, plus three minutes' walking. Is that okay?"

"What time is the bus before that one?"

He didn't have to think long. "Ten sixteen."

I looked at my watch. It was five after ten. "If we take that one, we won't have enough time to eat out."

Harold the Hawk nodded. He just stood there waiting for me to make up my mind. I wished it was more like the old days where maybe he would have pushed or manipulated me into saying to heck with the early bus, let's eat out.

I thought about it and about what Mom said, and then I thought this was my first real date out, and there was no way I was going to freak out about being home on time.

I grabbed his arm. "I'm hungry. Let's go eat."

I had a cheeseburger with a malt. Harold the Hawk had a nutburger with a coke. He asked me how I liked the movie, and I said it was neat.

We sat a while longer, and then Harold the Hawk picked up the check. "We'd better make that bus now. If I get home late, my mom will give me heck."

"Okay, Harold," I said. "I understand."

10

"Well, how did it go?" Chloris asked.

"Terrific," I said.

"How was the movie?"

"Wonderful."

"Did he take you out to eat afterward?"

"Marvelous," I said.

"*Yech!*" Chloris said. "I'm going to bed."

I couldn't sleep. I felt more like humming. Some of the theme music from *Star Wars*. *Da dum dum dum dum dum da dum.*

Mom got home looking tired.

"Well, how did it go?" she said.

"Terrific," I said.

"Were you home by eleven?"

"*Da dum dum dum dum dum da dum,*" I said.

"I guess there's no point in asking you about your homework," Mom said.

"Sensational," I said.

When I got to bed, I forgot how to sleep. I can understand now why some of those jet-set girls look so tired.

11

I got up early Sunday morning. Chloris was still asleep. Mom had already left for her gym where she works out with yoga and calisthenics, trying to stay in shape and fight off middle-age flab.

I do at least five miles on my run now, and hope to push it up to ten soon. They have mini-marathons in L.A. with courses ranging from 6.2 to 13.1 miles, which is a half-marathon. One day I'll be ready to enter one of them. Men and women compete. Boys and girls, too.

My running route is measured to exactly five miles. Up to the park, around it twice, back to our house, and once around the block. Mom and I clocked it off in her car and had to try several different routes before finding one that came to exactly five miles. To run ten, all I have to do is go around twice. And anything in-between is good for building up my endurance.

Running is what helped me get over my depression after Mom left Fidel. It got rid of the anger and the terrible feeling of helpessness that I felt. And after finding out I had unloaded my feelings, I discovered that I liked running. I ran more and more, and got better at it. My average time for a mile was down to nine minutes, not too bad for my age.

When I'm running, my mind detaches, and I can

think of things for a longer time, go over them again and again in my mind. This time, my thoughts were about me and Harold the Hawk, the nice feelings I had when I was with him. It was the discovery of a new me, a gentle me. A feminine feeling, I suppose, the kind I'd never had before.

I thought of how interesting it was that Harold the Hawk was trying to make real meals like Irish stew with dumplings, while I was still too lazy to go past making tacos or tuna-fish sandwiches. I decided to get out some of Mom's cookbooks and practice making dumplings. Then I could tell Harold how to make them perfectly instead of having them fall apart and spread all over the pot.

I decided, too, that Chloris was all wet with her advice about how to handle boys. There was no way I was going to play hard-to-get with Harold. Even though I had no experience with boys, I knew he was the right one for me.

My body was flying along with my thoughts this time. When I got back to our house, my watch told me I had done my best five miles ever. Instead of forty-five minutes, I had done it in forty-one!

I went inside, my chest heaving, feeling very good. Chloris was in the bathroom, doing her Sunday morning clean-up chore. I do the kitchen, floor and sink, and vacuum the rugs. Chloris looked up. "You had a phone call."

My heart was still thumping too hard for me to notice any difference. "Who was it?"

"Who do you think? Your weirdo friend."

All of a sudden, I wasn't dragging. "Harold the Hawk?"

Chloris made a wry face. "How would I know what his name was? How many weirdo friends do you have?"

"Did he leave a number?"

Chloris shook her head.

I sat on the rim of the bathtub. "Well, if he didn't leave his name or his number, how do you know it was my friend you call the weirdo?"

"He was breathing kind of funny," Chloris said.

"Like how?"

Chloris bent over. She went into a series of grunts. "Huh huh huh."

"Is that how weirdos breathe?"

"You'd better believe it. How else would a girl know?"

"Is that how your pepperoni-freak friend breathed the night he drove you home? You know, when he wouldn't let you out of his car until you kissed him good night?"

Chloris nodded. "Huh huh huh. They all breathe the same. I guess weirdos can't help it."

"Even after you kissed him good night?"

Chloris smiled, her green eyes gleaming. "Especially after. He'll be hung up driving girls home the rest of his life after that, trying to make it happen again."

"Trying to make *what* happen again?"

Chloris grinned at me. "You're so dumb, Jenny. Now I know you didn't get to kiss your weirdo friend good night." She saw me staring. "It rings a bell, dumbbell. That's why you kiss somebody."

I wondered if this was something like running where your body tries to tell you something. "What happens if the bell doesn't ring?"

Chloris shrugged. "Then you know there's nothing between you two people. No spark. No electricity. So you might as well forget about that person."

I got up off the rim of the bathtub. I knew Chloris knew more about it than I did, especially because I didn't know anything at all about it.

"What if one person's bell rings and the other's doesn't?"

"Same thing. Dullsville. One-sided is no good. It's got to be the same feeling for both."

"Gy," I said.

"Don't worry. You'll find out next time."

The phone rang. I didn't move and Chloris looked at me. "Aren't you going to take it?"

I shook my head.

Chloris laughed. The phone rang and rang and rang, and then it stopped.

"You're weird," Chloris said.

I shrugged. "It could have been for you, you know."

We looked at each other then and both laughed. For a brief moment there, Chloris and I were sisters on the same side, sharing the same feelings. It was a nice feeling, for a change. Even if it possibly cost me a call from Harold the Hawk.

12

Monday began like any other day. An overcast sky with the sun trying to break through. I was used to seeing that kind of day, and didn't pay it much attention. It was just another Monday. Back to school. Ho hum.

But it turned out to be different from the other overcast days, the other Mondays in my life. Or any other day.

It started to fall apart for me when I got to

school. At the far end of the hall ahead of me,
walking in my direction, was my Friday night date,
Harold the Hawk. There was a wide white bandage
around his head, almost covering his forehead.

That boy, I thought, isn't right for skateboards.
He's built to self-destruct.

The students in front of me drifted away, the
crowd thinned out, and I noticed Harold the Hawk
had something on his left arm. It looked like a girl
called Debbie Myer. She was walking so close to
Harold the Hawk, somebody might have thought they
were born Siamese twins. Either that, or Debbie had
somehow managed to become glued to his side.

I wanted to hide, but ours is a new school built
after the last earthquake, and there aren't any holes in
the walls. There weren't enough kids in the hallway
for me to duck behind, either. I thought of turning
around and heading the opposite way, but something
inside me stopped that idea.

So I kept walking toward them, trying not to look
at Harold and Debbie, my eyes fixed somewhere in
space, but somehow couldn't control my focus and
kept glancing at them. I was very close when I noticed Harold the Hawk was trying to be invisible, too.
"Oh, hi," I said as if surprised.

Harold's eyes weren't happy or surprised. "Oh,
hi." His body was tilted, half turned away. Debbie
Myer looked at me without any expression at all, or
rather a look that denies expression. A cool look that
Chloris does easily. It's part snooty, part disdainful,
part innocence. Like the cat-who-ate-the-canary look.
Who me? I didn't do anything.

Then I was past them, walking fast, feeling red-
faced, an empty hurting feeling in my stomach, as if I
hadn't eaten all day. That's what feeling a certain way
about a boy can do to you.

I suddenly wondered if Harold the Hawk had
ever let himself in for more girls like Debbie Myer,

waiting to crawl up his sleeve. It occurred to me that he knew an awful lot about making the right bus and movie on time for a boy whose main interest in life was supposed to be riding and falling off a skateboard.

To make matters worse, Debbie Myer was easily one of the prettiest girls in school. A real neat-looking girl, or so I had always thought until I saw her on Monday morning walking so close to Harold the Hawk Osborne. Now I didn't like her nearly as much.

I hadn't seen her out for the school track team or even out for volleyball or softball. She looked too sweet and delicate to be a skateboarder. You could tell from one look that if Debbie Myer ever fell down, she would wait for somebody to pick her up. And most of all, what I didn't like about Debbie Myer was that she appeared to be the type of girl who not only wouldn't mind being a boy's sex object, but expected it.

This thought really blew my mind because even though Harold the Hawk had told me his mother was a policewoman and seemed against sexism and appreciated women being valued for what they were, he might forget all the rules when he was with Debbie Myer, and treat her like they used to treat girls, by falling for her.

As a result of this kind of extreme inward feeling, I didn't do too well in the first study period, and spent more time worrying about Debbie and Harold the Hawk than I did in getting ready for my English class.

The bell sounded for the next class, and I went out in the hall. Naturally the first person I bumped into was, you guessed it, the boy whose mother was fuzz.

He was standing there all alone, just himself and his books and his ten-mile pack of bandages and gauze.

"Hi, Jen," he said, "how you doing?"

"What happened to your head?" I said.

"It was an accident my being there with Debbie Myer, you know," he said. "I hardly know her."

"She seemed to know you, all right."

"What happened was I tried a loop and crashed into a tree. I've got to practice my loops more or I'll be wiped out next week in the skateboarding contest."

"Have you taken her to any movies, Harold?"

"Who, me?"

"What's a loop?"

"You see, what happened was Debbie Myer works for the school paper. And she found out my mother was a policewoman and she wanted to get an interview with me about it. For the school paper, that is. The *Blazer*."

"I take it back. I don't care what a loop is."

"Oh, a loop isn't any big deal. You just go around and under. I mean, it's nothing compared to your running five miles, for example. Now that's really hard. Takes a lot of endurance."

"You really think so, Harold?"

"I sure do. I bet next year you're going to be right up there close to the winner of the mini-marathon."

"For your information, next year I'm going to win it!"

"Oh. Well, anyway. You're the only girl I ever took to a movie. We don't count home TV, do we?"

"What happened with home TV?"

"Well, my mom and I once visited my cousin Gloria and her folks. I watched a little TV there with her."

"Is she pretty?"

"I don't know. They don't get very good reception up in Bakersfield."

"Well, how long are you supposed to wear those crazy bandages?"

"She'd got blue eyes and dark hair like you. That's all I remember."

"When are you going to Bakersfield again?"

"Two weeks."

"And how long will you be there?"

"Huh? I'm not going anywhere. I meant the bandages are coming off in two weeks."

"You fall too much, Harold. Maybe you don't keep your mind on what you're doing. Was Debbie Myer interviewing you when you fell out of your loop?"

"It felt more like a tree. Listen, skateboarding isn't all that easy. You ought to try it sometime."

"No, thanks. Did they have to take any stitches?"

"No, it's just a road rash."

"What's that."

"Burns. Scrape burns."

"Well, I just wanted you to know I really enjoyed that movie with you, Harold."

"That's okay. You know, I wouldn't mind seeing it again."

"How come?"

"I guess I didn't see too much of it."

"Well, how come?"

"I was kind of worried my arm was going to fall off."

For some reason, both of us laughed then. It broke up all the crazy feelings I had inside me.

"You can watch TV over at our house some time, Harold."

"Well, I don't know," he said.

"How come. Too much homework?"

"No, I have to do a lot of baby-sitting."

I was about to tell Harold the Hawk that baby-sitting was girl's work. Then I realized suddenly that Harold was being brought up under the new rules by his mother the policewoman, and that all jobs are supposed to be equal, just like men and women, boys and girls.

"I do a lot of that, too," I said. "I baby-sit a lot."

"You do?" Harold said. "Hey, it looks like girls are getting into everything nowadays."

"You better believe it," I said.

13

Kathy Kingman, my best friend, called me in the afternoon, sounding happy and excited. "Guess what? We found an apartment."

"How neat! Where?"

"Beverly Glen in Westwood. We just moved in. The phone is in already."

"Beverly Glen isn't far. What number?" She told me where it was, a few blocks above Santa Monica Boulevard. "That's less than a mile away. Can I come over?"

"Well, why do you think I'm calling?"

"Hang up. I'm leaving."

Chloris wasn't home yet from school. I left her a note and took off. Beverly Glen is a steep curving hill. Harold the Hawk would have given a lot to skateboard down that hill.

The apartment building was one of those new security types with locked gates and doors. If you didn't have a key, you had to be identified and buzzed in. To get identified, you had to dial the number of the apartment you were visiting. I had forgotten to ask. Kathy probably didn't understand the rules of her new apartment building.

I hung around getting madder and madder at the dumb building. There was just no way to sneak in. Nobody came along who lived there that I could follow inside. There was an underground garage and that had a security gate, too. It was a large building with too many windows to wave at and hope to get Kathy's attention.

I finally figured to heck with it and was about to go back home when Kathy came down. "I forgot you couldn't get in. Have you been here long?"

"About a hundred years. Why did your mother pick such a dumb building?"

"She said it was safer. Everybody is moving into security buildings these days. People are tired of being mugged."

"Well, nobody has mugged us yet. If you ever lose your key here, you could starve to death outside."

Kathy looked around. "Yeah, I guess. Well, come on up and see it. We're still unpacking."

"Okay."

As we went into the elevator, Kathy looked at me. "You grew a lot since the last time."

I shrugged. "I couldn't help it, Kathy. It just happened."

A year ago, Kathy and I had been nearly the same height. She was stocky and I was the thin type. Now I was at least six inches taller, and it seemed Kathy hadn't grown at all, not even an inch. The trouble was that she was very self-conscious about it.

She made jokes like "Well, at least I won't have to worry about being too tall." Or "Anyway, now I won't have to play pro basketball." And "If I was taller, I'd be all spread out. This way I think I can concentrate better."

I knew it bothered her. Her ex-father Mr. King-man was a tall man, and her mother was tall and slender, too. It was about the only thing I didn't like to talk about with Kathy. I think she was afraid she would always be as small as an eight-year-old child. Or a ten, maybe.

"Maybe I can get a job in a circus," she said once.

I didn't get it at first. "Doing what?"

"Playing the Girl Who Forgot How to Grow."

Kathy's mother had taken her to a few doctors. They didn't know what was wrong. She'll probably grow out of it, they said.

As we rode the elevator up, I tried to slump down a little. "Are there any boys in this building?"

"I don't know yet. Here we are—tenth floor."

The apartment was very large, a big living room with a terrific view of the streets below. People and cars looked so small. "Everybody looks so tiny," I said like a dumbbell.

Kathy laughed. "That's why we moved here. To make me feel at home."

"Gy. You'll grow out of it. Remember what the doctor said."

"He said 'probably,'" Kathy said. "Come on. I'll show you my room."

Her room was cluttered with boxes all over the bed and floor. The windows faced to the rear of the building, north.

"I can see the mountains from here," Kathy said, "when there isn't any smog."

I looked and couldn't see any mountains. "Yeah. Well, Anyway it's good to know they're out there."

I helped her unpack some boxes while she put her clothes away in the closet and her chest of drawers. She held up a short red skirt. "My father got this for me for my last birthday, my twelfth. What do you think he sent me this year?"

I couldn't guess. She went to her desk, and

opened a little box. She took out a small envelope and pulled out a card. It said "Happy Birthday, Daughter."

"Well, at least he remembers you're his daughter," I said.

"Yeah. Too bad he forgot the date. He sent it a week after my birthday."

"That's okay," I said. "It's still better than nothing."

"You mean Fidel forgot yours?"

I shook my head. "He wouldn't forget. He explained it to me once. About his other daughter, his real one. You have to learn to let go, he said. Otherwise you keep all those feelings alive that you have to forget."

Kathy sat down on her bed. "I don't see why. Why do we have to forget?"

"Because otherwise you can drown in your sorrow and self-pity, Fidel said. I think he was right. I feel a lot better now that I've nearly stopped thinking about him."

There was so much to remember about Fidel, I wondered if I would ever forget him. He made me always feel good, like I was something special. He once said I was his sunshine.

When Mom wanted her divorce, he didn't put up any fight. He didn't get angry and yell about it like Kathy's father. He just said he was sorry it hadn't worked out. He told me not to feel too bad, not to worry, that some day I would have a new daddy to love.

I could picture him now in his big studio in the old house in the canyon hammering away at his large paintings, or carving up some gigantic log he had brought home for sculpture. I could still remember how I felt sitting on the high wooden horse he had made for me, feeling the horse would take off, fly right out the studio windows into the sky with me on its shining back.

Kathy's voice woke me out of my spell. "Hey, you okay?"

"I was thinking about Fidel again," I said.

"He still lives at the old house. I've seen him a few times. He waves. I think he's lost a little weight."

I picked a shoe up from the carpet. "Where does this go?"

"Throw it in the corner. That's my undecided section. Is your mom dating again?"

"Not yet. I think Chloris has her faked out and she's afraid to try any new guys. She thinks that maybe this way Chloris will love her again."

"Rotsa ruck," Kathy said. "What's new in your life?"

I tried to make it sound cool. "I had a date with a boy from school Friday night. He took me to see *Star Wars*."

Kathy whooped and clapped her hands. "It's a big breakthrough for us. Your very first date, right?"

I nodded, feeling warm and flushed. "Well, yeah."

"Terrific. Did he take you out afterward? I mean, did you go any place?"

"There's this place to eat across from the movie. Ship's. We didn't have much time. My mom told me to be home by eleven."

"How was the movie?"

"He was real nice," I said. "A little nervous, but okay. I expected to be nervous but I wasn't."

"Did he fool around? In the movies, I mean. With his hands?"

I remembered Harold the Hawk groaning after he put his arm over the back of my seat. I didn't think that counted. "No, I don't think so. If he did, I didn't notice, Kathy."

"Yeah, sure. Is he nice? Are you going to date him again?" She threw herself back on her bed. "Wow! This is exciting! How old is he, this boy?"

"His name is Harold Osborne. He's about fourteen, I think."

"Is he tall?"

"Kind of. He rides a skateboard a lot. He's trying to be world champion, or something."

"Is he good?"

"Well, yeah, only he falls a lot."

"They're always falling. All that showing off. They scare me. They come zooming up right behind you and turn around on it—"

"Fiip-kick," I said.

"Whatever. Does he stand on his head on it, too, like some of the nuts I've seen?"

"I haven't seen him do that yet. But come to think of it, his head is always bandaged. Did I tell you his mother is a policewoman?"

Kathy looked interested and surprised.

"He does the cooking because she works. He makes dinner."

"He sounds interesting. What else does he do?"

"Baby-sitting. I don't know all that much about him yet."

Kathy got up and opened a big box. "Help me put some of this junk away. Then we can watch some TV."

"I think I'm in love, Kathy."

She stopped moving. "Are you sure? On only one date?"

"I saw him walking with a girl today at school. I got so jealous I wanted to kill him. My stomach hurt like it was on fire. I thought I would explode inside."

"How does he feel about you?" she asked.

"I don't know. I mean we only just met recently."

"Did he try to kiss you good night when he took you home?"

"No."

"How come?"

"I don't know. We had to rush home to get there

on time. Him, too. His mother didn't want him to be
out late."

Kathy frowned. "You should have kissed him.
You should have found some way to kiss him."

"Why?"

Kathy smiled. "So you could tell me what it's
like."

"Well, maybe it will happen some day. Then I'll
tell you about it."

"Yeah, but hurry it up, huh."

"You'll probably kiss somebody before I do,
Kathy. There probably are a million boys in this
apartment building."

"So what? They won't know I'm alive."

"Some day you'll probably get stuck in the elevator with one of them. By the time you get out, you'll
probably have a boyfriend."

"That's a way, all right. As long as they can't get
away."

"Maybe you ought to get yourself a skateboard.
Go where it's really at. You can probably meet a lot of
boys on a skateboard. Don't forget I met Harold the
Hawk that way. I mean I was jogging, but he was
riding his board."

"It's a thought," Kathy said.

"Only you have to expect to fall a lot, get those
road rashes and bruises. I mean, before you get real
good at it."

"It sounds as if you have to be real dedicated to
go through all that," Kathy said. "I don't know if I
could be that dedicated."

"Well, yeah. I'm into running now. I can be really
dedicated about that."

Kathy looked very impressed. She asked how far
I was running now and I told her my latest distances
and the times. "Next year I plan to enter the city
mini-marathon," I said.

"I've got to find something that I like to do like
that," she said. "But I don't think I like running, and

I'm not all that sure about the skateboarding." She clenched her fist. "I know I've got to get myself into something, and stop going around like a sad sack."

"I can ask my friend Harold about what kind of board you would need," I said.

"Tell him I'm the fire-hydrant type. Maybe that would help him pick the right kind for me."

"Oh, come off it, Kathy. You'll grow. You know you will."

"How do I know I will?" she said.

"Well, everybody does. You're only thirteen. You're not a hundred years old, you know."

"What if I'm still the same way when I am a hundred years old? Or maybe I'll shrink and be a full-time dwarf."

"Well, look at me," I said. "What if I keep growing and I wind up ten feet tall?"

Kathy thought about it. "You'll be tall, all right. You could play basketball. They would call you Too-tall Jenny." She laughed. "What's Chloris like?"

"She's very pretty. And she has a perfect figure already. Like she could be Miss America some day."

"You mean she's that beautiful?"

"If she isn't already, the way she's going, she will be."

"You mean perfect, except for what's inside her head."

"Yeah. She's not dumb. She only thinks dumb sometimes."

"Boys don't notice that. Boys like them to be dumb," Kathy said. "Haven't you noticed that?"

"Well, not really. So far this is my first experience."

"How about your friend Harold? Hasn't he noticed yet that you're not dumb?"

I shrugged. "He doesn't know much about me yet."

"Maybe that's the right approach. Keep them guessing."

"I don't like that approach, Kathy. I know I wouldn't like him to keep me guessing. I would get so jealous I could die."

"If you're that jealous, it means you really are in love."

"It does?"

"Everybody knows that. Because otherwise, you wouldn't get upset about anything."

I realized that now two people had told me I was in love. I wondered if Harold the Hawk was going through the same experience.

14

Everything was going along fine. Mom seemed happy about her job and came home on time. Chloris kept doing her part-time job at Patsy's Pizza, did her homework, and didn't act snotty toward Mom. She helped me with my own homework. She was too good to be true. I kept telling myself this couldn't last, that something was brewing, that any minute there would be a big explosion in the Carpenter family.

Just the same, when it came, I wasn't ready for it.

It started when one Sunday Mom said she had a date for dinner and hoped Chloris and I wouldn't mind eating by ourselves. She told it to me, and I walked into our bedroom and passed the news on to my sister.

"Some new weirdo," Chloris said. "I figured he was about due. It's been too peaceful around here."

"Maybe he's okay," I said. "Anyway, what's the difference? There's nothing wrong in a woman wanting a date out with a guy."

"She's not a woman," Chloris said. "She's a mother. Mothers aren't supposed to step out on dates with guys."

I looked at her. She was serious, her face set into her former lines of anger. "What's being a mother got to do with it?" I said. "We're not babies anymore for her to take care of. And she's not married. She's free to do what she wants. What would you do in her shoes?"

"I wouldn't be a two-time loser, I'll tell you that. I would stick to the first man I loved and married." She was reminding me again of the so-called bad deal Mom pulled when she divorced our original daddy.

"You don't know that for sure," I said. "Anyway, suppose he got sick and died or had an accident?"

"Same thing," Chloris said. "If he dies, it's all over for both of us. I don't go out looking anymore. I stay home and take care of my kids."

"Okay. What if they grow up, what's she supposed to do then? Keep sitting around waiting to die?"

Chloris got up and threw a pillow violently against the wall. "I wish she would," she said harshly. "I wish she would just do that and get it over with. I'm getting sick and tired of her going out with weirdos."

"You're crazy," I said. "Anyway this is her first date in a long, long time."

"I wouldn't bet on it," Chloris said. "She doesn't tell us everything she does."

"She doesn't have to. Why don't you want her to have a good time?"

Chloris' eyes were shining as they do when she becomes excited. "Because she doesn't deserve a good time," she said fiercely. "She's got to be punished for what she did. For when she dumped and divorced Daddy. She has to pay for that."

I shook my head. "You're weird. A lot of people get divorced. Some get married again. Some don't, not right away anyhow, and keep on dating and looking. Like Kathy's mother. I loved Fidel but I don't care if she gets married again, or dates some guy, or even a lot of them. Didn't you ever hear of Women's Lib?"

"Well, sure. What's that got to do with her?"

"You're not for real. The whole thing is that now women can do whatever they want to do with their lives. Just like men. They can do whatever they feel like. Also get the same jobs as men for the same pay, and so on."

Chloris waved her hand. "Oh, I know all about that jazz. I've heard some of those women talking on TV. They want to be like men. Well, I've got news for them. I don't want to be, and nobody's going to tell me what to do."

"It means being equal. Chloris."

"Maybe," she said. "But I don't want Women's Lib telling me how to go about it, how to run my life."

I remembered that I had a difference of opinion with Women's Lib, too. I couldn't blame Chloris for having her own objections.

"Well, anyway," I said, "there's not a heck of a lot you can do about it. If Mom wants to date somebody, it's her own business, not yours."

Chloris stared at me, white-faced. Her green eyes were gleaming. Her whole body became tense, rigid. "You think so? Well, you've got another think coming. And so does she."

I began to laugh nervously. "Why? What are you going to do?"

She thrust her face close to mine. Her fists were

closed tightly, the knuckles white. "I'll leave, that's one thing I can do. I can run away."

She was so intense and serious about it, she frightened me. "Oh, Chloe, come on. You wouldn't do that."

"Oh? Wouldn't I?"

She stalked out of the room then without another word or glance. I stayed there as if petrified. I knew her temper, and that Chloris was capable of doing nearly anything when she was crossed or upset. She wasn't the type who could let anything affect her and make her feel unequal. She had to take a stand and fight back.

It's the Scorpio way. They don't sit and take it like other people. They plot and plan and make you pay for what you do to them. It's their particular kind of pride. Somehow they manage to get revenge for even a fancied insult.

All I could do now was hope for the best. That it would all blow over. But at the same time, I knew hoping alone wasn't going to do it. Chloris wouldn't let anything blow over. If you did anything to her, she made you pay for it. It's her nature and the Scorpio way. Scorpios have to win.

I sat down to think. Mom is a Taurus, a very stubborn type. There was no way anybody could talk to Mom and tell her what to do, either. Taurus is the sign of the bull, and they're not kidding. A bull keeps coming on and coming on until somebody kills him. He doesn't know what it means to stop, think it over, or take a step back.

Like Mom.

She hadn't let our first daddy stop her from having the kind of life she wanted, and divorced him right after Chloris and I were born. She loved Fidel but when she became upset with him and he wasn't making her as happy as she wanted to be, she dumped on him, too.

So there was little to hope for thinking that Chloris would understand Mom or that Mom would bend or give an inch to Chloris and what she wanted.

I was the only one who could switch from side to side, like a true Libra tyring to keep things at a steady balance. But I was the only person whose opinion nobody cared about.

I had half a mind right then and there to call my friend Harold the Hawk to get his thinking on what was going on in the Carpenter house. But then I realized nothing had really happened yet, that it might never happen, that so far it was really only all in my mind. So I didn't call him.

But I thought it was very interesting that I *thought* about calling him!

15

By six o'clock Sunday evening, Mom was showered, perfumed, and all dressed up. She was wearing a new blue dress and dark blue shoes. Her long black hair was brushed thick and glossy. Her lips were smiling, glistening with deep red lipstick. She had on a lot of makeup and mascara accented her dark blue eyes. She looked terrific.

"How do I look?" she asked and before I could answer, she walked happily past.

I realized suddenly how the idea of going out on a date with a man transformed Mom into almost a different person. She became more alive, vibrant, happier. Most of the time she acted anxious and worried, grumpy and impatient, complaining about this or that. I wished that Chloris could see the difference in her now, and not begrudge her the times when she had a date with a guy to look forward to, and came alive and feminine again.

It was clearly obvious that Mom liked men, and thought they were important enough for her to dress up for and to change her personality. Maybe it was anti-Women's Lib, but it seemed more natural for her, and I liked it.

My first movie date with Harold the Hawk had given me nearly the same feeling. Like I was better than myself, all charged up inside, almost flying out of my skin. It was a super feeling, and I hoped he would always be there to make me sparkle. He gave me a strange kind of inner excitement, something I had never felt before. Maybe I was beginning to experience a changing sexual growth. Whatever it was, it felt good, the way I would like to feel always.

Sunday evening was a night off for Chloris at Patsy's pizza joint, Monday the other. Sunday nights usually were for catching up on our homework, watching TV, doing our hair, washing and ironing our personal stuff for the coming school week. Dinner was over by seven, as a rule, and there would be the whole evening ahead of us. Time to prepare next day's lunch, yak on the phone with friends, maybe try baking a new kind of cake.

Sundays were usually our best family evenings at home, and I wondered now what Chloris would do when Mom's new date showed up.

I was on the living-room sofa watching some early TV news. Mom came out of her room and sat down beside me to do her nails. Chloris walked out of the bathroom, went to the hall closet, and took out her windbreaker. "I'm going out," she said.

Mom stopped buffing her nails. "Where are you going?"

"Out," Chloris said. "Out."

"I'd rather you didn't," Mom said.

Chloris turned, undecided, the coat half on. "Why not?"

Mom got up. Because I want you here when Mr. Sloan arrives."

Chloris shrugged. "What for? I'm not interested in your company."

"I know," Mom said tautly. She walked a few steps closer toward Chloris. The happy, smiling look was gone. Her eyes were hard, her voice sounded harsh. "I want Mr. Sloan to meet my family. You and Jennifer. After we leave, you can go or do whatever you please. But I want you here until he comes."

Chloris hesitated. Her voice rose as she pulled the windbreaker off. "Big deal. Why do I have to hang around to meet one of your new weirdo friends? After him, there'll only be another one and so on."

Mom took another step forward and slapped Chloris hard across the face. Suddenly she was yelling: "My friends are not weirdos! You'll show some respect for them and for me."

Chloris reeled back and fell against the wall. She looked frightened, her eyes rolling. Then she shook her head angrily, and began to yell, too: "Why should I? They don't mean anything to me. No more than you do."

Her words seemed to hang in the air, frozen and locked in space. It was as if you could look up there and read them. Mom's mouth opened, and she looked shocked. A fleeting expression crossed Chloris' face, as though she was surprised herself at her own words and wished them back.

Mom recovered first. "I'll try to forget that you said that, Chloris." Her voice became quieter, more bitter. "If meeting my friends is so difficult for you, go ahead and leave. I wouldn't be proud of introducing a daughter of mine who feels that way about me."

Before Chloris could answer or do anything, the doorbell rang. I looked at Mom but she waved me off and went to the door herself. She opened it and a tall brown-haired man came inside. He smiled down at Mom. "Hi, Marge," he said. "Sorry if I'm late."

Chloris was staring at him, her lips parted with surprise, and I couldn't blame her. Mom's date, Mr. Sloan, was so handsome, so terrific looking, he seemed unreal in our apartment. He looked like a movie star.

Chloris looked at me, and we exchanged silent thoughts. I knew she was thinking exactly what I was, and I smiled at her. Chloris drew herself up and gave me her cool look of disdain, but she didn't fool me. I knew she felt like a dope after what she had said.

Mom closed the door and leaned against it, her head back. "Hello, George. I wanted you to meet my two daughters. This is my younger one, Jennifer—"

"Hi," I said goofily, as if I was four years old.

"—and this is Chloris." Mom had a small mocking smile on her face. "She was just leaving."

Mr. Sloan tilted forward toward Chloris. "Oh, too bad. I had hoped to get better acquainted. A heavy date, I guess?"

Chloris looked up at him uncomfortably. She shook her head, tossing her hair back with a quick gesture. "N-no, well, not exactly." She lifted her windbreaker. "Nothing that important. Just leaving."

Mr. Sloan nodded understandingly, and kept smiling. He was very tan. He was wearing a gray suit over a blue shirt and red and blue tie. His black shoes were shining. He had a big gold ring on a finger of his right hand and a gold wristwatch on his left wrist. I noticed he also had cuff links with red stones. I wondered if they were rubies.

"Well, too bad. Next time, then," he said.

Chloris was stuck now. I could tell she wanted to stay a while longer and talk to Mr. Sloan. But in her

own mind she was still carrying on her fight with
Mom. She tried to slip her jacket on without looking,
getting the sleeves all fouled up. "Aghhh," she said.

Mr. Sloan stepped closer quickly. "Allow me," he
said. He turned the windbreaker right, and then held
it out for Chloris. She stared wordlessly up into his
face and got into it. "There you are," Mr. Sloan said,
still smiling. "Looks mighty good on you, Chloris, I
must say."

Chloris looked over at me, then at him, then at
Mom. She pushed her hair back, and got her poise
back. She nodded coolly to him, giving him the prin-
cess smile she practices in the mirror, and walked
slowly to the door. "Well, have fun, you guys." She
half-turned to glance at Mom, as she went out.

She had not yet walked out the door completely
when Mr. Sloan said to Mom, "Well, you do have a
beauty there, don't you, Marge." He saw the door
close in his face, then turned and noticed me again.
"Yes, another pretty one. Jennifer, eh? Do they call
you Jenny?"

"Nope," I said, feeling stubborn for some reason.
"It's the whole thing—Jennifer."

"Oh. Well, fine. I'm delighted to meet you, Jennifer." He looked at Mom. "About the same age as my
little girl, Marge, don't you think?"

"Jennifer is thirteen," Mom said coolly. She
picked up her wrap. "All right, George. I'm ready."

"Oh," Mr. Sloan said, looking surprised. "Oh, fine."
He got the door open for her, and stepped back for
her to go through first. But Mom had her own ideas.
She sidestepped and faked out Mr. Sloan so he had to
leave first. Then she turned to me. "Good night, Jenny. Don't wait up. I'm locking the door." She pushed
the automatic lock button in, and went out pulling the
door behind her. I heard Mr. Sloan's voice, very
friendly. "Good night, Jennifer. Nice to have met
you."

I didn't answer. I watched the door close. Then I

went to the window and waited. They had a lot of steps to walk down before I heard a car engine start. I waited and then I heard a key turn in the lock. Chloris walked in. She pushed her hair back and looked at me. "Well, what do you think of him?"

I was shaking my head. "Weird," I said. "Too friendly."

Chloris grinned. She puffed up her chest, lifted her shoulders, and began to strut across the room. She was giving a pretty good imitation of Mr. Sloan.

"Well," she said, sounding like him, "you do have a beauty there, don't you, Marge?" She threw her arms out and whirled around the room repeating it over and over. "Well, you do have a beauty there, don't you, Marge? Don't you, Marge? Well, Marge, do you or don't you, Marge?"

She finished with her face practically into mine, and I had to back off laughing. But she had more to say in her imitation. "Allow me," she said. She grinned idiotically. "Allow me! There you are! Looks mighty good on you, I must say. Har-umph—yes, mighty good."

I laughed again and fell into my sister's mood. "I'm de-lighted to meet you, Jennifer. About the same age as my little girl, Marge, don't you think?"

"He's a creep," Chloris said.

"He's a freak," I said.

"A real phoney," Chloris said.

"A weirdo," I said.

Chloris clapped her hands, her eyes gleaming, smiling triumphantly. "I told you."

It had all happened so fast, I thought at first she had trapped me. Sucked me into her viewpoint. I was about to shake my head no, I didn't mean it, but something nagged at me that maybe she was right this time.

"He was really laying it on," I said.

Chloris nodded. "What a line of bull! Acting like we were a couple of dopes."

"Gy," I said, "how can Mom fall for that stuff!"

Chloris shrugged. "I guess you'll do anything if you get desperate enough."

"Well, anyway, you got to admit he was good looking."

"Sure he was. So what? After you finish looking at him, you still got to listen to him, don't you?"

"He looked like some TV actor," I said.

"He looked like a real jerk," Chloris said. "In fact, the more I think of it, I think he's more of a jerk than a weirdo." Chloris glared at me, losing her gay mood. "Okay, you said it was okay with you whatever she wanted, whoever she picked, right? You mean to tell me you'd want a jerk like that hanging around here all the time for a new father?"

I hesitated. "It was only a date. How do we know she wants to marry him?"

"That's not the point, dumbbell," Chloris said. "The point is, if she does something dumb like that, we're the ones who'll have to live with it, right?"

I thought about it and slowly nodded. "I guess so." Chloris threw her head up and turned away, knowing this time I was in agreement with her. I wanted to be fair about it, see both sides evenly, but there just wasn't any argument here. Chloris was right. Too bad, Mom, I thought. This time you goofed. Fidel was a real person. You never should have left him. Now it's not just Chloris. It's the two of us against you.

16

Mom sat down for breakfast the next morning. She wasn't sparkling anymore, but then she never does at that time of day. It was a work day, and she's always girded up long before she ever gets to Bontel's.

"Well, how did you like Mr. Sloan?" she said.

I shrugged, stirring my oatmeal. "He's okay, I guess."

Mom was looking directly at me, noticing that I was avoiding her glance. Chloris had already left for school and was safely out of it. "He has very nice manners," Mom said. "You must have noticed that."

"Uh huh," I said.

"And I think he's quite a handsome man. Don't you?"

"He's okay," I said, shoving oatmeal into my mouth.

Mom was into a fried egg with her coffee, and now she stopped and put down her fork. "I suppose that's your way of telling me Mr. Sloan didn't impress you, Jenny."

I was getting nervous and a little angry. It was her affair, wasn't it, not mine. "I said he was okay. He's your friend, not mine."

Mom was angry now. "I see," she said. "I suppose I'll have to put every man I meet to a vote here, to see how you girls feel about him."

59

It struck me that this was a good idea, but I knew it would never come to pass. Mom was being sarcastic, not realizing or caring that Chloris and I would have an opinion regarding whomever she dated.

"Do we have to talk about him?" I said uncomfortably.

Mom looked at her watch and folded her arms. "Yes, that's not a bad idea. I suppose you and your sister spent your time having a good laugh about your mother going out with a younger man."

I stared. "Gy, we never even noticed that. Is he?"

"A few years, but it's not important," Mom said. "What is important around here is the attitude of you girls. What did Chloris think about him?"

"Why don't you ask her?" I said, finishing the last of my oatmeal. I got up to rinse the dish off in the sink.

Mom's voice had the old-time harshness in it that she usually reserved for Chloris. "Oh, so now you're siding with her."

I put the dish under the hot water. "It just worked out that way," I said. "We didn't plan it."

"What way?" Mom said.

This time I looked at her. I had to raise my voice because the water was making so much noise. "He was too polite. Too smooth. He treated us like a couple of dopes. We both thought he was a phoney. A real jerk."

It was one of the few times in my life that I ever got something off my chest like that to Mom. In a way, I was sorry the moment the words came out of my mouth. And yet in another way, I felt good about it, that she had cornered me and prodded me into telling how I felt. Till that moment it had always been Chloris and her at each other, since my original daddy killed himself. I always managed to stay out of the arguments. With Fidel, I had good reason to speak up and tell her what I thought, and yet I hadn't. Now for some reason, I wasn't holding back. I was telling it like it was.

Mom looked surprised, and then almost ready to cry. "It was only his first visit," she said, her voice shaking. "You only spoke to him for a moment. How can you tell what kind of person he is, based on that?"

"I don't know what kind of person he is," I said. "All you had to do was not ask me. You asked me, so I told you what we thought. He wasn't for real. Maybe it's like you said, that it's his good manners. But we—I—thought he was phoney. Putting it on like he did."

I was wiping my dish so hard it slipped out of my grip. It fell to the floor before I could grab it and broke. I went down on my knees to pick up the pieces. "Stupid dish," I yelled.

"Careful of your fingers," Mom said.

I got the broom and swept it up into the dustpan and dropped it all into the trash basket. I was still shaking and mad. I threw down the towel on the drainboard.

"You didn't finish your milk," Mom said, pointing to the half empty glass.

"I don't want any milk," I yelled. "Good-bye. I'm gonna be late for school."

When I came out of my room with my books, Mom was still sitting there. "You're sounding exactly like your sister now. I thought you were different."

"Maybe I am," I yelled. "Only next time don't bring home any weirdos."

Talk about words hanging there! These filled the whole kitchen. I could hear the electric clock ticking and a slow drip from the water faucet.

Mom sat there looking stunned.

"I'm sorry," I said. "I didn't mean it. Honest, I didn't. It just came out. You're right. We didn't talk

with him long enough to know him. Maybe he's nice
when you get to know him."

I went over to kiss her good-bye. Mom's cheek
was wet.

17

I felt awful all the way to school. Ashamed and
guilty. Mean and rotten. All those things. I felt two
feet tall.

Yelling at Mom, being impatient with her, were
things I had never done before. Something was happening to me that I didn't understand. It was as if I
was turning into another Chloris.

Whatever it was, I knew that I wasn't the same
old evenly balanced Libra I always had been. That I
was supposed to be, according to the astrological
signs. I had to wonder now about this, about how
reliable astrology was. I didn't have the real know-
how about computing my chart to find out what was
wrong. All I knew was that something was fouled up
somewhere. Maybe Saturn was hanging over me, giving me a bad trip, but I suspected it was more than
that.

My disposition was changing, for sure. Could I
lay that on a planet millions of miles away? I was
becoming involved in new things, in different ways.
Arguments were things I had always avoided. I had
always taken it for granted that my sister Chloris was

the pill, and I was the good one. Yecchh! I thought.
Goody Two-Shoes!

A secret part of myself that I never knew was
there was coming out, surfacing, forcing me to look at
it. It was a meaner side. A look-out-for-yourself side.
When any problem had come my way before, I
had avoided it, managed to duck it or not face it
squarely. Now it was as if I didn't want to do that
anymore.

Maybe I was growing up, I thought. The idea
was new. It scared and depressed me. What did I
know about growing up? I had been a little girl for so
long that I was used to that. It felt so much safer.

Harold the Hawk was waiting outside for me
when I got to school. He was looking down at his feet,
raising up and down on his toes. Practicing nose-
wheelies for his best friend when he got home.

I felt better seeing him, at first. But then I realized he was a boy, a new boyfriend, another thing I
didn't know very much about. I could see where
growing up, while very interesting and a lot of fun,
could also be a big pain. You had to fake it a lot. Be
careful you didn't get dumped on.

I watched Harold going up and down, wondering
if Chloris was right about him and his board. The
trouble I might have with it on our honeymoon. Was
she psychic?

He saw me, glanced at his watch and came
up, grabbing my arm. "Hey," he said smiling, "did
your bus driver try a different route? You're four
minutes and thirteen seconds late."

I looked down at my arm. His hand was still
there, and as I kept going, the rest of Harold the
Hawk went along with me.

"I'm sorry, Harold, I don't feel much like laughing or even talking. I just blew my stack at home with
my mom."

"You did?"

"Yeah. So if you feel like talking, okay. I'll listen."

"It's nothing to get paranoid about," he said. "I blow my stack a lot at home."

"You do?"

"Sure. But my mom is kind of cool about it. She knows I don't really mean it. Like when she jumps all over me on something. I don't let it get me down. I know she doesn't mean all that, either. It's cool that way."

I nodded. "That's a pretty neat arrangement, anyway."

"Sure. Also, by the time she gets home for dinner, it's out of her mind already. So many other screwy things have happened to her since. Usually things that are a lot more important."

"What do you blow your stack about?" I said.

"A lot of dumb things. Most of the time, it's because of some new guy she's starting to date. Some jerk I hate."

I had to laugh. Harold the Hawk looked down at me, surprised. "That's exactly what happened with me! She asked me what I thought of her new guy that she dated last night. My sister Chloris and I hated him on sight. So I told her."

"Before she went out with him?"

"No, later. Today. This morning."

"Hey, that's heavy," he said. "What was wrong about him?"

I shrugged. "Well, for one thing, he was awfully good-looking."

Harold the Hawk nodded sympathetically. "Yeah, that's rough."

"And he was too polite, you know. Said all these good sweet things, like how adorable my sister and I were, how terrific it was for him to meet us, and so on."

"Jerk," Harold said.

"Yeah, well, now I'm not so sure. I mean, like my mom said, how could I judge him on that short meeting? And there's nothing wrong with having good manners. I mean, he didn't do anything wrong. He was simply trying to be friendly. Only we thought he overdid it."

"Well, sure. They all do, you know. If they're wise, they know right away that we're the enemy."

"We are?"

"Of course. We're still hung up on our own parents. We're afraid somebody else is going to take them away, take away the love we used to get. We don't want to lose it."

I stared. It had never occurred to me that boys thought about these things. The idea of either Chloris or me worrying about losing Mom's love was something else that hadn't entered my mind. If that was a fact, it could have explained a lot.

"Are you sure about that?" I said.

"I heard it on a TV program about stepparents. There were a couple of shrinks and a couple of parents, into new marriages after divorces, with new kids from the other's spouse. All kind of mixed up, you know. And that was the main idea they put across, that the kids are afraid of losing the love of their natural parents and so they act up, act as rotten as they can to bust it up."

I squeezed his arm, and nearly died when I realized what I had done. Anyway I was happy. "I'm sure glad it's the word of an expert instead of just yours, Harold."

"Well, I'm kind of an expert, too, you know. My parents split when I was eight. I've had five or six years' experience behind me in dealing with my mom's new dates. I could have told those shrinks a few things."

"Such as what?"

"That it changes sometimes. Sometimes you get

to like the new guy, and then your parent decides that she doesn't. Then you're hung up hating her for not picking the one you finally wanted."

"Gy," I said.

"How you coming with your running?"

"Okay. How are things between you and your best friend?"

"Terrific. I'm into vertical rides now. I carved a pool over the weekend. Being high on the wall is a full-on rush. Just like surfing—only more intense. I only had two falls."

Listening to Harold the Hawk was like taking a new course in a different language. Here we were nearly the same age, going to the same school, and I could only guess at some of the words he was using.

"What's a vertical ride?" I said.

He showed me the wall. "Like that. We go straight up."

"How do you get down?"

He spun around, arms raised. "Nose-lift and kick-turn."

"What's carving a pool?"

"Making my own tracks, on a pool."

"Don't you get wet I mean when you come on down."

"These are dry pools, Jen. It's what we're into now. It started with the Dogtown guys. Riding pools and pipes."

Dogtown was another name for Santa Monica. Not too far away. "What's a full-on rush when you're high on a wall?"

He beat his chest with his fists happily. "It's a gas!"

"How come you don't talk English?"

"Oh, that. My old lady rides me about that, too. But it's part of the skate scene. You come along with me some time, and you'll talk funny, too. All the kids do. Also you may wind up liking it a lot. Tail-tapping a pool-rim wall is super. I bet it'll grab you."

"Well, maybe," I said. The school bell rang. Kids began falling into groups and lines, going inside.

Harold the Hawk leaned close. "Hey, what are you doing Friday night?"

"I don't know. Why?"

"I got to baby-sit. I thought maybe you'd like to come on over and sit with me."

"Well, I don't know," I said. "I think I might have a baby-sitting job myself Friday night."

"What do you get?"

"A dollar an hour," I said.

Harold the Hawk frowned. He shook his head. "That's wrong, Jen. You're not taking inflation into account."

I'd never thought about inflation. Only about making a few bucks of spending money for baby-sitting.

"My rate is a dollar thirty-five," he said.

"They pay you that much?"

"They pay more," he said. "They find it's easier to figure out at a buck and a half."

"Gy!"

We had to separate and go to different classes. But I had discovered something meanwhile. So far, Harold the Hawk was turning out to be the most interesting person I knew.

Dr. and Mrs. Klugherz were sure going to be surprised to learn my rates for baby-sitting their kids had just gone up.

Inflation can be a neat idea, too.

18

Harold the Hawk had zapped my mind. I went around to my classes feeling warm, full of bubbly good feelings. Hours after he had left me, I could still feel the touch of his hand on my arm. I found myself rubbing it gently as if I wanted to seal it in. That was a new weird feeling for me.

I wondered if it was the same with him. If he could still feel his hand on my arm. It was a disturbing thought, because I knew that if I asked him, and he said no, he didn't, I would feel crushed. I didn't want to ever feel that let down. Especially not after feeling so high and good about something.

What he had told me about his experiences with his mother and her new boyfriends churned inside my head, too. I could hardly wait to get home after school and tell Chloris what he had said. How we were determined to hold on to our loved ones. Not willing to accept any change such as a new stepparent.

She was standing in front of her mirror practicing her put-down look. A lot of the models you see in the ads are doing that now. They look right at you as if they don't see you. They're supposed to be modeling a new hair lotion or a dress or cigarette, but their expression is take it or leave it, as if they don't care whether you like the product or not. They look surly or sullen, but most of all what they don't do is smile. The new models today would rather be caught dead than show a smile or look happy about anything. Most of them. Chloris had been doing that look naturally for a long time, before the models ever thought of doing it, and they had never heard of her.

"That's a good look for putting out the garbage," I told her. Then I went into what Harold the Hawk had said.

Chloris listened with no expression. "That's bull. So far I haven't seen anything but weirdos. Why can't she find a normal guy?"

"Well, maybe she'll come up with one some day," I said.

Chloris patted her fingers over a bored yawn. "I can hardly wait."

The phone rang. Usually I'm in the habit of answering it whenever Chloris is around. The younger sister slave type, you know. But this time I figured the heck with it. I sat back on my bed and let it ring.

Chloris looked at me. "Aren't you going to answer it?"

"I don't hear anything. I got deaf all of a sudden."

"It might be your Harold the Hulk," she said.

"Hawk."

"Huh?"

"Harold the Hawk."

The phone kept ringing. She looked at me impatiently.

"Maybe it's your pepperoni-pizza freak. Or some other weirdo you know."

Chloris glared. Then she flounced across the room and picked up the phone. "Carpenter residence," she said. A wry expression showed she was let down. "Oh, hi. Yeah, we're home. Yeah, the homework is fine. Do you want to talk to Jenny?" She grimaced, bobbed her head, and rolled her eyes at me while she listened. "Yeah, okay. Okay, I'll tell her. She just got home. It's okay. We'll figure out something to eat. Yeah, okay. Good-bye."

She hung up and threw herself back on the bed. She lay there looking up at the ceiling. Her lips were set tight

"It was Mom, huh?"

Chloris lay there without answering, ignoring my question.

"Is she working?"

Chloris curled her lip. "Working? Sure. That's what she said. We know it means she's got another date with some guy."

I shrugged. "Okay. So what?"

She didn't answer.

"So what?" I said. "What's the big deal if she does?"

Chloris didn't answer and kept staring up at the white ceiling. She appeared to be troubled in her silent thoughts and was shaking her head, turning it from side to side. Her bored-princess look was gone now, that get-lost-don't-bother-me-look. She had become vulnerable now, and there was a look of pain etched on her face. Her lip trembled, and she was clenching her hands into fists.

She made a soft moaning sound. "I don't know. I don't know."

I couldn't believe she was so genuinely affected. "What difference does it make?"

Her voice rose. "It makes a big difference. We're her family. She's supposed to think of us first."

"Oh, come off it," I said. "Big deal. We're not babies. We can make our own dinner. If you're too tired, I can do it."

"That's not the point. You don't seem to get the point."

"Okay. What's the point?"

Chloris sat up. Her face was pale and set coldly

now in anger. "One of these days, I'll show her. I won't come home either. See how she likes that."

"Gy," I said. "What for?"

Chloris leaped to her feet suddenly as if I'd stung her. "I'm tired of her taking me for granted," she shouted. "If she's going to be a part-time mother, I can be a part-time daughter."

"You're weird," I said nervously. "Where would you go?"

"Wherever I feel like."

She looked so cold and determined, she scared me. "You don't want to do that, Chloe. There's a lot of real crazy people out there. Los Angeles is full of them. They got all these stranglers and rapists and fiends. It's all over the papers and on TV."

Chloris gave me a thin cool smile. "So what? I'm not afraid of them."

She had me really worried now. The newspapers were full of stories and pictures of a lot of terrible things happening to young girls on their way home from school or work. Sometimes from hitchhiking with strangers.

A recent picture from the news flashed into my mind. A young girl found facedown on a dirt road in the hills who was strangled, badly beaten to death. I began to cry. "You wouldn't do that."

She looked at me fiercely. "How do you know that I wouldn't? I've got a job. I can support myself."

I saw her through my tear-blurred eyes and hated her for scaring me this way. "You do that and I'll never talk to you again," I yelled. "I mean it, too."

Chloris smiled. "I don't have to go away by myself, either, you know. My friend Wayne has asked me to go away with him."

I stared. "Away? Where?"

"Some weekend. Skiing. Up at Mammoth Mountain."

I stared some more and gulped, unable to think of what to say. I didn't know if she was telling me the truth, or putting me on.

"You're making that up," I said angrily.

"Am I?" She smiled and looked at herself in the mirror again. "Well, I'm not going to do it tonight." She looked at me in the mirror. "I thought you said you were making dinner."

I rushed past her furiously to get to the kitchen. It was the old Scorpio hub-and-wheel effect again. But it was much more than that. Chloris knew me, that I would do anything for her. She could always wrap me around her finger whenever she wanted to.

I yanked the taco shells out of the fridge container, still trembling. I was so mad and crazy, for a brief moment I hoped I would make something so rotten that she would get sick eating it.

That's what loving a person too much can do for you.

19

Dr. Klugherz' wife called me later to ask if I could sit for them Friday night. I remembered Harold the Hawk asking me if I was free Friday night to baby-sit with him on his job. But I knew I would feel silly doing that, so I never took his offer seriously.

"Could you make it early, Jenny," Mrs. Klugherz said, "about five-thirty? We have to eat early to make a show."

"Sure," I said. "There's just one thing. I'm asking more money now for baby-sitting."

"You are? How much?" She didn't sound happy.

"A dollar thirty-five an hour."

"A dollar thirty-five? How did you arrive at that figure?"

"Inflation. You know."

She hesitated a moment and I wondered if I had priced myself out of a nice job. I liked Dr. and Mrs. Klugherz and their kids. Their place was always clean, she left me stuff in the fridge to eat if I got hungry, and Dr. Klugherz always drove me home. That crazy Harold the Hawk, I told myself, why did I listen to him? A dollar an hour isn't bad.

But she recovered her sense of humor soon enough. She giggled and said, "It's all right. I just remembered my husband raised his office-calls rate, too. It used to be nine, now it's twelve."

"Twelve dollars? Gy!"

"Well, you've got to remember doctors have to pay a lot for office rent, equipment and nurses," she said. "You don't have that kind of overhead, Jenny."

"Yeah, I know. So it's okay?"

"Of course. And good for you! It's about time we girls began fighting for what's due us."

I made a mental note to take back what I thought about Harold the Hawk raising my price because of the inflation. "What time will you be home, in case my mom wants to know?"

"About twelve-thirty. I'm not sure when the show breaks."

"Okay. See you at five-thirty then."

"Fine, Jennifer. Thank you."

I hung up and began multiplying. Six hours at my new rate would give me eight dollars and ten cents. Wow, I thought, I'm rich!

Chloris passed by. "Did I hear you telling somebody your baby-sitting rate was a dollar thirty-five an hour?"

I nodded, smiling. "That's right. For Dr. and Mrs. Klugherz. She said it was okay."

Chloris stared. "How come you picked that number?"

"Inflation," I said.

"Huh?" she said. "Oh, yeah, that's right." She went to the table, grabbed my pencil and started making her own calculations. She threw down the pencil, frowning. "Darn that pizza place! If they gave me thirty-five cents more an hour, I could make a dollar seventy-five more a night. That's almost nine dollars more a week."

"Sure," I said. "But you've got to remember pizza places have to pay a lot for rent, equipment and cooks."

"What equipment?" she said angrily.

"Well, like the pots and pans. The silverware, napkins. The glasses. Salt and pepper shakers."

Chloris tossed her hair. "Are you for real? That stuff is already there. How often do you break a pot or pan?"

"Okay. How about the food. That costs them, right?"

She sat looking at her figures unhappily. "Yeah, I guess. The trouble is I don't know how much."

"Well, thirty-five cents an hour isn't that much, either. Mrs. Klugherz said okay right off."

"Yeah, but he's a doctor. They're rich."

I shrugged. "Maybe if you ask for thirty-five, he'll give you twenty-five anyway."

She grabbed the pencil again and began figuring. "Well, that's not too bad. Six and quarter for the five days. It's an improvement, anyway."

"Well, yeah," I said. "Only what if he won't give it?"

"Why won't he?"

"I don't know. He has other help, too, hasn't he?

Plus the cook and dishwasher. What if they all want more?"

Chloris angrily hit the table with her fist. "Well, that's got nothing to do with me. That's his problem."

"Maybe you ought to find out first what the other kids are getting."

"There's only Janie and Debbie waiting on tables, besides me. I know what they're making. Same as me."

"Unless they already asked him for the raise and got it," I said.

Chloris glared. "They would have told me." She stopped and thought for a moment. "Anyway, I think they would. But I don't care. I'm going to ask for more. If he doesn't pay me more I'll find another job."

"Gy," I said. "I thought you liked working at Patsy's. With your pepperoni-pizza freak coming there often and all."

"So what?" she snapped. "He's not that important. But making more money is."

"How come?" I asked.

She tossed her hair and looked off. "You know why. Just in case, if you want to really know."

I stared. "You mean about leaving here—going away—?" I was so upset I couldn't even finish my sentence.

Chloris got up. "It all depends, you know. Like I said." She looked at me threateningly. "But you better not say anything. This is strictly between you and me."

She walked out, leaving me alone with my thoughts.

20

Harold the Hawk was outside school again Tuesday morning. He seemed to be waiting for me. He also seemed to be doing something peculiar with his feet. Bending his toes down, then up.

"What's that one called?" I said.

"Gorilla grip. You do it barefoot I like your hair."

"Why?" I said.

He shrugged. "I saw this girl doing it. Her toes hooked right over the end of her board. Good for a nose-wheelie."

"I mean, why do you like my hair?"

"Oh," he said. "I guess I like to see it all brushed out and long, that way."

"Do you? That's nice," I said.

"I wonder if I can get some extra points for doing a gorilla grip," Harold said. "You ought to wear it that way more often."

"Okay, maybe I will," I said. "I took your advice on the baby-sitting rate, Harold. I'll be getting the same as you Friday night. One thirty-five. Thanks for the tip."

"I think it's terrific that girls can do so many different things with their hair."

"You do?"

He nodded. "That's much better, you know. On an average four-hour job, you'll be making a dollar forty more an evening. Figure one a week through the year, you'll be making seventy dollars more."

"I guess so," I said. "I didn't bother figuring it that far in advance. I didn't know you were an expert on hair."

He grinned. "You don't have to be an expert to know what you like. Anyway, you have to know your growth rate in relation to the current inflation figures plus depreciation."

I noticed it was very difficult to keep Harold's mind on one single track. Every time it came around to me, it was as if he switched trains. "I don't have to care about depreciation just yet, Harold. I'm only thirteen years old."

"Well, in two more years, you'll be in high school. You won't be that interested in baby-sitting. You'll be going out on dates. That's a kind of depreciation."

"I will? I mean, it is?"

He nodded. "So you have to figure how many years you have left for it."

"Well, baby-sitting isn't all that important to me, Harold. I can think of better ways to spend my time."

"Well, yes. But in a few more years, you'll be going to college. Carrying a heavy load of homework and be even more interested in dating. You won't have much time for baby-sitting then at all."

"That's okay, Harold. I really don't care that much about it."

He blinked. "I kind of like those wedgies you're wearing, too. Are they comfortable to wear walking?"

I wiggled my toes. "Very."

"Of course, there are other jobs you can get," he said. "How are they about walking up and down stairs?"

"They're okay," I said. My feet felt too big, all of a sudden. "My sister has a pretty good job. She works at a pizza parlor part-time, as a waitress. Sometimes she makes a lot of tips." I wondered if this was the night Chloris was going to ask Patsy her boss about her raise. And then I wondered if he would give it to her. And then I wondered if she really meant what she told me.

"—the stress factor," Harold was saying.

"I'm sorry, Harold, I missed that."

"I was talking about the stress of the tip factor. It's variable, you know. All your sister can depend on is the minimum hourly working rate. That's only a dollar seventy more than your new baby-sitting rate."

The school bell rang. I wanted to ask him so many things. I wanted to tell him about Chloris and her job. Her pepperoni-pizza freak. Her free ride home where she had to kiss the guy to get out of the car. I wondered if Harold the Hawk had already thought about that, and didn't want me to get a job where I had to kiss a guy to get a free ride home. "Are you going to be a banker when you grow up?" I said.

"I don't think so," he said. "I don't think that dealing with figures is all that exciting."

"Well, you seem to be handy with them," I said. "You have everything figured out."

"That's true," Harold said. "But figures—numbers, time schedules and like that—those are things I can work with. You can move them around and see where you are. I don't have any control over anything else. Everything else is very iffy."

"You do all right talking about your skateboarding, too," I reminded him. "You and your best friend."

Harold the Hawk nodded his head a few times. "You have a point there, too. My board isn't as dependable as figures, but it gives me something else to work on."

We were walking through the hallway having this very weird conversation. When we came to the junction where we had to separate to go to our respective classes, Harold said, "I can be flexible about a few things. What would you like to talk about, Jen?"

I blurted out the words without thinking, "Well, there's us, you know. You and me. You're my first boyfriend."

Harold the Hawk nodded some more. He looked very serious. "All right. That's a thought. You're my first girlfriend, too. Maybe I've avoided talking about us because I'm afraid."

"Afraid of what?" I said.

"Well," he said, "for one thing, girls are something I don't know anything about."

"Okay," I said. "I feel the same way about boys."

"No kidding?" he said.

"No kidding."

Harold the Hawk smiled and rumpled his hair a lot. "Hey, that's terrific," he said. "I need the money, but I kind of wish I'm still clear Friday night. I'd much rather keep you company while you baby-sit. It has one built-in advantage I see right away."

He worried me saying that. "Like what?" I said.

Harold the Hawk shrugged. "Well, we save a lot of time and money not going out."

21

Harold the Hawk called me at home right after school. "My people cancelled for Friday night," he said. "So what do you think?"

"What do I think about what?"

"About my coming over on your baby-sitting job."

"Gy, I don't know. I'll have to ask Dr. and Mrs. Klugherz."

"Oh, they know me. I've had him for a couple of sore throats. I've also done some baby-sitting for them when the kids were younger."

"Well, just the same," I said.

"Okay. Sure."

"Also I guess I'll have to ask my mom."

"Well, I don't know her," Harold said.

"Maybe she won't mind. I already told her your mother is a cop."

"Policewoman," Harold said.

"Well, yeah. Incidentally, how does she do on runaway girls?"

"How do you mean?"

"I mean, what happens if she finds them, if she does?"

"If they're under fifteen, she brings them back home."

"What if they're over?"

"I think after they're fifteen or sixteen, they don't have to go home if they don't want to."

"Are you sure?"

"No. Are you asking in regard to your sister?"

"No, I'm just asking."

"Well, I'll ask my mother."

"What happens if they don't want to go home? Where do they go?"

"Some kind of juvenile home, I think. But the judge and people down at Juvenile Hall decide on what happens. They talk to the runaway girl and the parents, you know."

"Can they run away if they want to even if things at home really aren't that bad?"

"Well, sure. What's not bad for you or me might be terrible for somebody else, boy or girl."

"Will you ask your mother about that, too, please?"

"Okay. When will you know about us and Friday night?"

"I don't know."

"I'll keep it open at this end, just in case."

"Well," I said. "That's up to you."

"I don't get it," Harold said. "You said you wanted us to talk about each other. I guess that means getting to know each other, doesn't it?"

"Yeah, I guess."

"So my keeping you company Friday night would be a way, wouldn't it?"

"Sure," I said. "But there's another way, too, you know?"

"What's that?"

"Going out again on a date."

Harold was silent for a moment. "You mean another movie?"

"Whatever," I said.

"Hey, that's a thought," he said.

"If you're broke, we can go Dutch," I said.

"Hey, that's a thought," Harold said.

"Anyway, I'll see you tomorrow."

"I hope so. These calls cost money," Harold said.

22

When I got home from school, Chloris was already there. As a rule, I'm home about an hour before she is. It bothered me a little but I didn't understand exactly why until I noticed that she was looking at herself in the dresser mirror, trying on a new short leather coat. She turned from side to side, trying it with the collar up and down. Then she tried it with her hands in the pockets. She stood there that way staring intently at herself, ignoring me.

"How come you're home so early?" I said.

She kept her eyes on her reflection, turning to face herself three-quarter view, one foot pointed out, the model pose. "I cut a class. Big deal. I had some things to do."

"When did you get the coat?"

"Do you like it?"

"It's okay. When did you get it?"

"The other day. They had a sale at the May Company. I like it. It's warm."

"How come if you got it the other day, you didn't try it on sooner? You never wait that long to try on something new."

She laughed as if amused. "Okay, you're right for a change. I picked it out the other day. I only just picked it up there."

My eyes must have widened. "You bought it for yourself?"

"Sure. Why not? I'm working, aren't I?"

Chloris probably didn't realize how cheap and tight she had become since she started working and saving her money. I had an allowance too, which I was putting in a savings bank along with my baby-sitting money. But we only spent our own money on little things, records, junk food, like that. When it came to clothes, Mom always got them for us. Sometimes her mother, Grandma Grace, got us stuff we could wear, usually for birthdays or on Christmas.

"I thought you were saving all your money for college," I said.

Chloris shrugged, still eyeing herself, and pulled the collar down, turning to face herself from another angle. "Yeah, but so what. It's still a long way off. Meanwhile I wanted this."

"How come you didn't ask mom to buy it for you?"

She faced me then, her eyes angry and gleaming instantly. "Because she wouldn't have. I know her. She would have told me it's not practical. Or that I got other coats like it."

I stepped closer to feel the material. It looked like leather only it wasn't. "Well, you do, sort of. What kind of stuff is it, imitation elk?"

"I don't know," Chloris said. "The girl told me it was water repellent, anyway. I don't have one like that."

"How much?"

She opened the belt and drew it tightly around herself. "Guess."

"Four ninety-five," I said.

She laughed mockingly. "Twenty-five ninety-five is more like it. Marked down from thirty-three."

"Gy! That's nearly what you make all week at Patsy's."

She smiled and threw her head back. "So what? It's my money. I can decide whether to spend it or not."

I was trying to think of an answer to that when the phone rang. This time Chloris didn't try to out-wait me but dashed across the room to get it.

"Carpenter residence." She frowned as if disappointed and held the phone up. "It's for you. Kathy."

I picked it up from her hand. "Hi, what's cooking?"

"Do you mind if I come over? I'm going crazy here all by myself."

"No, come on. Do you know how to get here?"

"Not exactly. Give me some directions."

I told her how to come. "Figure about fifteen minutes. We're on the first floor all the way around to the right. Apartment one-oh-four."

"Okay. I'm on my way."

No sooner had I hung up than the phone rang again. I handed it to Chloris. "This one is probably for you."

She grabbed it and sat down on her bed. "Hello," she said, making her voice soft and sexy with just that one word. I heard a guy's voice from the other end. "Oh, hi," she said. She looked up at me suddenly and frowned. Then she picked up the phone and walked across the room with it. It has a long extension cord, and she said, "Just a minute," to him before walking out of the room and closing the door behind her.

I got the message. It was a personal call, and she didn't want me to listen in. That was okay, or would have been, ordinarily.

But this time I suddenly became uptight and wanted to listen. For one thing, it might be her pepperoni-pizza freak, Wayne Gavin. The guy who had given her the free ride home which only cost her a good-night kiss.

For another thing, she had already told me she might go away with him some weekend to go skiing up at Mammoth, the big snow resort area up north.

For a third thing, she had already bought the car coat, or coat which would be just right for the kind of weather they would be having up there.

I had three big things to bother me already, and then I discovered that I had a fourth. That I didn't like this guy Wayne, not at all. Somehow I didn't trust him.

And also now I was afraid Chloris might do something crazy, and I didn't trust her anymore, either.

23

When the doorbell rang, a little later, I went to answer it, and Chloris, still talking on the phone, went back into our bedroom, closing the door behind her.

Kathy came in shaking her head. "What kind of a building is this, anyway? You walk right in without any security gates, no buzzing or anything."

I laughed. "You still having trouble with yours?"

"Somebody ought to shoot the guy who built it. Even when you manage to get in, the dopey elevators don't always work. Do you know what it feels like to walk up ten floors?"

"Gy! How often does that happen?"

"Twice so far, and remember we only just moved in. The security gate doesn't always open when it's supposed to. Or sometimes people calling buzz, and you don't hear it upstairs so you don't buzz back to open the door for them. They call you from the corner drugstore to tell you what a dumb building you live in, as if you didn't know it already."

"Well, maybe you'll move to another building," I said.

"No way," Kathy said. "We signed a two-year lease."

"What about the boys in your building? Did you meet any yet?"

"I've met a few, either too young or too old. The

only one my age is built like me. Who needs any more like that?"

"So what? If he likes you and you like him is what's important, Kathy. You shouldn't be going around measuring people."

She nodded. "I know. I'm getting a terrible complex about it, too. I keep imagining that everybody else in the world will grow except me. Even little babies just being born now will grow up and pass me. Like I'm the only human being stuck in time and space. That's pretty wild, isn't it?"

I was trying to think of a way to turn her off that kind of talk when Chloris came out of her room. She was humming happily, still wearing her coat.

"You remember Kathy," I said.

"Sure." Chloris came over to where we were in the living room. She was smiling, in a good mood. "You still living up there in that weird canyon, Kathy?"

"No, we just moved back to Westwood, on Beverly Glen."

"Terrific," Chloris said. She looked down at Kathy with a critical eye. "You've grown a little, haven't you?"

"No," Kathy said. "I haven't. I'm still waiting for it to happen. Is that a new coat? My mom's got one just like it."

Chloris preened hearing that. Kathy's mother is not only young but she's terrific looking, a real dingaling.

Chloris spun around. "Like this?"

Kathy nodded. "Exactly. Real Uruguay leather. It cost over three hundred dollars."

"Well," Chloris said. She looked at her wristwatch. "I've got to go out for a while. See you guys later."

"Mom comes home at six," I said warningly.

Chloris looked at me. "I know. Don't worry."

I was at the side window looking through the curtains almost as soon as the door closed. I didn't see Wayne Gavin or anybody who could have been him waiting there.

"What are you looking for?" Kathy said.

"A car."

Kathy looked puzzled. "What kind of car?"

"One with a pepperoni-pizza freak inside."

"Huh?"

I let the curtains fall back into place. "Well, he could be waiting out front for her."

"Who?" Kathy said.

"I can't tell you yet," I said.

"Okay," she said. "Hey, what's happened to Chloris anway?"

"What do you mean, Kathy?"

"I mean, how did she get to be so beautiful all of a sudden?"

"I told you last time, remember?"

"Yeah, I know. But I didn't believe you."

"Remember last time when I told you I thought I was in love?"

"Yeah. You mean with your skateboard friend?"

"Yeah. Harold the Hawk."

Kathy laughed. "I like that name. Do you still feel the same way about him?"

I nodded very positively. "Even worse. Or better."

"Terrific," Kathy said. "How does he feel about you, the same way?"

"I think so," I said. "But he used to kid a lot, and now he's very serious."

"What's he serious about?"

"He worries a lot about money."

"You mean he's cheap?"

"No, I don't think so. Just careful."

"Well, has he taken you out since that movie?"

"No. But we're working on it."

"That's good." Kathy was silent for a moment. "Last time when you visited me, you said I ought to get into something, remember? To get out of myself?"

"Well, yeah, sort of."

She took a folded piece of paper out of her pocket and passed it across to me. I looked at her mystified. "I'm writing poetry now. Maybe this way I'll get it out of my system."

I unfolded the paper and read it. It was a very short poem.

Growing Up
by
Kathy Kingman
The thing I think most often of
Is growing up to be a dwarf.

I shook my head and folded it back together. "Oh, Kathy."

She took another from her pocket. "This one is funnier, I think."

Tall Beats Small
by
Kathy Kingman
Little people don't have fun
With taller people
All around,
The only time we get the sun
Is when the taller ones
Are done,
I've found.

I folded this one, too, and handed it back to her

"Well, what do you think?" she said. "You can tell me."

I shook my head, unable to speak.

"Look at it this way," Kathy said. "I am getting it out of my system, aren't I?"

24

I didn't bother asking Mom if it was okay to see Harold the Hawk on my baby-sitting job with the Klugherz kids. Somehow I made up my own mind that it wasn't such a hot idea. I know a lot of kids date that way, but it didn't seem right for me. Maybe I was afraid to be alone with him. And no doubt if what Harold was telling me was true, his mother would be afraid for him to be sitting there alone with me! So either way, I think I came to the right decision.

It was raining the next day when I got to school, and I didn't expect him to be waiting outside practicing gorilla-grips or tail-wheelies on his imaginary board. He wasn't and I was disappointed. I didn't think getting wet was nearly as dangerous as doing all those radical things around the rim of a dry swimming pool, carving his tracks in a full-on rush, or whatever it was he said he did.

I went inside and heard my name called. Turning, I saw Harold running madly through the rain, zigzagging and jumping to avoid puddles. I guess skateboarders don't like to get their feet wet if they can help it. Maybe it's why they use dry pools.

His landing foot skidded under him as he leaped

over the last puddle, and he nearly totaled himself right in the school yard. But somehow Harold the Hawk recovered his balance, and I guess by now he's used to falling mainly on his board. He came up to me looking pleased and excited.

"It's only a little puddle of water, Harold," I said. "You couldn't drown in it if you tried."

He shook his rain off his head. "It wasn't that," he said. "I was practicing jump-overs. You know, pretending my board was there under me waiting for me when I landed. It always skids out from under me when I land."

"What do you jump over?"

"Tables, mostly. The board goes under it while, I go up and over, and I'm supposed to catch it on the other side."

"I'd like to see that some time," I said.

"Dr. Klugherz has a good long coffee table," he said. "I could do it over that for you. Falling on a carpet isn't bad."

"No way," I said. "I don't think that's a good idea, your helping me baby-sit, Harold. I decided against it."

"You did?"

"It's just not a good idea."

"That's funny," he said. "It's just what my mother said. She wasn't all that happy about you and me being alone in somebody else's apartment."

"I think your mother, being a policewoman and all, has seen too many crimes, Harold. What does she think I'd do to you?"

He shrugged, not at all embarrassed. "I don't know. Maybe it's like you said. She's seen too many crimes. Of passion, that is."

"Passion? Us?"

Harold nodded, looking very serious. "You'd be surprised at the statistics, Jen. There are an awful lot of weird and sick people out here in L.A."

"Well, I'm not weird or sick," I said. "Tell your mother I'm only thirteen."

"I did," he said. "She said she wasn't worried so much about you being thirteen as she was about me being fourteen. Whatever that means," he added after a moment.

"Huh?" I said.

Harold took my arm with his wet hand. "You know," he said. " Right now you and I are both virgins, right? Well, one of these days, maybe, we won't be able to say that."

"In Dr. Klugherz' apartment? While I'm baby-sitting?"

Harold shrugged. "You never know, Jen. These things happen all of a sudden, I hear. Why do you think so many teenage girls are becoming pregnant?"

"From baby-sitting?"

"Look at it this way," he said. "A lot of teenage girls do a lot of baby-sitting, don't they?"

The school bell rang and we started walking down the hall again. I wondered if Harold had a point about teenage girls and baby-sitting.

"Well, I don't think we have any problem about that, Harold. If you remember, Dr. and Mrs. Klugherz agreed to give me more money for baby-sitting."

He scratched his head with his free arm that held his books. "Oh, yeah, that's right. What about it?"

"So I'd have to give even more attention to my job. That means, I might not even know you were there."

He nodded, pleased. "Hey, yeah, that's right. You would have to do that."

"It's your own fault, Harold," I said. "You talked me into asking for more money per hour. Now I've got to work harder for it. You just talked yourself out of a terrific chance of making me pregnant."

Harold sighed, seemingly relieved. "Oh, boy. I've got to remember that to tell my mother."

"How about teenage girls who go to movies?" I said. "Do you have any statistics on that?"

Harold shook his head. "Not offhand. I'll check with my mom."

"I'm not doing anything Saturday night," I said.

"Six forty-two," Harold said. "I'll pick you up at six forty-two. There's a bus at six forty-eight. The movie at the Crest starts at seven seventeen. It's over at nine twenty-two. We'll have more time to eat."

I looked at Harold. He seemed serious. We were at the end of the hall, at the point where we usually separate to go to our separate rooms.

"Hey, did you plan all this?" I said.

"Listen," he said. "There's only so much you can do with a skateboard. I mean, your fun is limited. And what happens when my trucks break or my urethane wheels fall off?"

"What are trucks?"

He waved his hands. "The metal gizmos that hold the wheels to the board and allow you to turn by leaning."

"How often do they break?"

"Well, not too often. But it's always a possibility. I've got to prepare for a more dependable and possibly more rewarding relationship."

He left me then, looking cool and happy, swinging his arms, not even waiting to hear if I said it was okay. I stood rooted there a long moment watching him, feeling very good about everything all of a sudden.

I could have called after him, told him, yeah, it's okay, Harold, I'll be ready. But I didn't. It was more fun being a love object in case Harold the Hawk's metal gizmo trucks broke or his urethane wheels fell off.

It was almost like being manipulated.

25

Craig Culbertson is our English teacher. He's young and very good-looking, has blue eyes and long blond hair and a droopy blond mustache. His voice is very soft and difficult to hear, and the kids like him because he acts sort of shy and not like somebody in charge of putting things into our heads. Some days we hardly get any work done because Mr. Culbertson likes to discuss things, not jump to any false conclusions, and sometimes the whole period can pass and we haven't jumped to any kind of conclusion at all.

Mr. Culbertson says not to worry about it, and that we'll table the subject for the time being and get back to it some other time. As a rule, we don't because something else happens and we get to discussing that one back and forth, and when nothing is settled, then we have another one to table.

In Mr. Culbertson's class, we have a lot of unfinished stuff lying around we can always get into, in case we have nothing to discuss at the moment.

Women's Lib was one of those, along with rock music, astrology, meditation, environmental improval, drugs, and government interference in the private lives of citizens. It doesn't seem to have much to do with English, but Mr. Culbertson doesn't think that's too important as long as we can learn to exchange views, and learn to live with antagonistic attitudes from others. Of course, he gives us readings from

93

selected authors he likes, and books for us to read, and there are topics he likes us to write on to get the idea of expressing our views completely before we become dominated by others with differing opinions.

This day I was thinking about my six forty-two date for the coming Saturday evening with Harold the Hawk, and my mind somehow got away from Mr. Culbertson and our English class. I heard somebody behind me hiss my name and saw Mr. Culbertson tapping his desk with a pencil looking straight at me.

"Are you there?" he asked me. "I've called your name three times."

"Gy, I'm sorry. What about?"

The class tittered. I looked around at them wondering what was so funny. Nobody bothered explaining, either.

"The question was," Mr. Culbertson said, "have you decided yet on your subject for an essay? We're trying to get an idea of what everybody will be writing about, to avoid duplication and make things generally more interesting."

"I don't know yet," I said. "Does it have to be serious?"

Mr. Culbertson shrugged. "Not necessarily. But my suggestion to the class, if you remember, was to pick something that would have meaning when related to our personal lives."

"Well, gy," I said. "That sounds serious."

"Not necessarily, Jenny. Think about it."

I thought about it. "Okay. How about skateboarding?"

"Skateboarding?"

I nodded firmly. "That's it."

"Skateboarding is meaningful to you?" he said. "Are you a rider yourself?"

"No. No way," I said.

"Meaningful and related," Mr. Culbertson said. "Does it fit there?"

"Yeah. Well, sort of," I said.

He continued to look puzzled. "Are you a viewer? You like to watch skateboarders, is that it?"

I shook my head. "No. I don't know that much about it."

Mr. Culbertson turned his hands over. "I don't get it. What's the connection?"

"Women's Lib," I said.

Some of the kids laughed and Mr. Culbertson pushed his droopy mustache around. "By way of skateboarding?"

"Call it the skateboard connection," I said.

Mr. Culbertson stared. "I hope one of us knows what we're talking about."

"Monday," I said. "I'll know more about it by Monday."

"Good," he said, not sounding too pleased. "For the rest of you, I expect at least five pages of good solid thinking and writing about something you genuinely feel has affected your life one way or the other."

Myra Englehorn raised her hand. "Is it okay if I write about my mother's divorce?"

Mr. Culbertson nodded. "Certainly, Myra. I can see easily where something of that nature could have a traumatic effect upon you. Divorce is fine."

Patrick Farley's hand shot up. "Hey, that was my topic. I was writing about our divorce, too."

Mr. Culbertson pushed at his mustache. "It's true, Patrick, that we wanted to avoid duplication, but perhaps Myra's essay on her family's divorce will be different from yours." He waved his hands. "You know. Different people, different children. Different problems."

"Anyway, mine is different," Myra said. "This is our second divorce."

Mr. Culbertson nodded and looked at Patrick. "Well, there you are," he said.

Patrick Farley looked mad. "So what? Big deal. So is ours."

Mr. Culbertson looked uncomfortable and cleared his throat a few times. "Are there any others here with experiences of a second marriage and new stepparent?"

Three other kids raised their hands, and mine went up, too. Mr. Culbertson looked shocked. "Oh, my! I didn't realize what I was getting into." He waved the hands down. "I'm sorry. I should have known better."

Some kid in the back of the room yelled, "Lots of us have two. Maybe somebody here wins with three."

Christine Anderson's hand shot up. "I got three. So far anyway."

The class buzzed with laughter and excitement. A boy I never liked, Philip Coles, raised his hand. He's always whispering behind his hand and pretending he isn't. "I got three if we're allowed to count live-in boyfriends."

Mr. Culbertson frowned as the class roared. "Now, now. Let's not have this thing deteriorate—"

"If we count live-ins, we win with six," Ellen Kester yelled. She was counting on her fingers. "No, make it seven!"

"You can't count live-in boyfriends or girlfriends," Sarah Turnbull said. "Only stepparents. Mr. Culbertson asked specifically about new stepparents. Otherwise, who could keep count?"

The other kids were jumping around, yelling, waving their hands. Mr. Culbertson looked upset. "Now hold it," he said. He hit his desk a few times to get their attention. "There's nothing funny about this. Divorce is not funny. People get hurt. It's not one-sided at all. It's tough on everybody."

"We're not hurt," Sarah Turnbull said. "It's fun.

Nobody stays around long enough, so you don't get to miss them."

The class cheered Sarah. I looked around. Everybody was excited and laughing. Mr. Culbertson looked very pale and determined.

"No, no," he said. "You're all wrong about this. Marriage is a serious thing. And so is divorce. Perhaps even more serious." He took a quick breath. "Everybody concerned has to recover, and start all over again. I hate to discourage all this enthusiasm. But still—"

The class continued to laugh, talking to each other. Mr. Culbertson looked at me. It was as if, in a way, I had started it all.

I shook my head. "I'm all recovered," I said. "After a while, you get used to it, Mr. Culbertson. Honest." But no sooner were the words out of my mouth than I thought of Chloris. "I mean, nearly everybody I know does."

Mr. Culbertson nodded the least bit toward me, as if he heard but didn't believe it. He banged against his desk again to get the class quieted down. "I can't believe what I'm hearing today. I've changed my mind. Anybody who wants to write about the separation in his or her family is free to do so. I don't care about possible duplication now. I'm more interested in sharing your experience."

The class hummed and buzzed some more.

"I'm not fooled by any of this," Mr. Culbertson said. "There still may be some here who have had, or are still having, great difficulty in adjusting." A couple of the kids snickered. "Perhaps some of you are putting on a big show for their benefit. When I read your papers, I may be able to learn what you really feel."

He was looking at me again. I shook my head. "No way," I said. "I've had it and now I'm out of it. I don't think it was funny. But I'm nearly all better, and I don't want to go through my divorce again."

Mr. Culbertson nodded with understanding. "That's perfectly all right, Jennifer. I don't see any point to reopening old wounds, either. As a matter of fact, I'm rather interested in your topic, and how you propose to tie up skateboarding with the idea of Women's Lib."

I waved my hands. I couldn't think of anything to say. The way nearly everybody had laughed and kidded about the divorces in their families had me shook up. I wondered what Harold the Hawk Osborne would have said to Mr. Culbertson on the subject of divorce. I imagined he would have made it all very reasonable about his mother beginning new relationships, without tearing her down and kidding about it.

I don't think he would have let those other kids kid him about it. I thing Harold the Hawk might have got very radical if they did, and socked somebody.

26

Harold the Hawk was waiting for me after school. It was still raining, and he was standing under a narrow overhang, his windbreaker collar turned up, rain dripping down on his wet head.

"What are you doing there?" I said. "You're getting soaked."

"It's okay," he said. "I was afraid if I waited in the hall, I'd miss you coming out some other door."

He fell into step beside me as I headed for the

line of kids waiting for the bus. "After I spoke to you, I suddenly realized I hadn't asked if you wanted to see that particular movie. If you don't, there's another one that got pretty good reviews, but we'd need to meet at a different bus time."

"What's the one you picked?"

"*Turn-off*. It's the one about the sniper at the ballgame—and he loses his contact lenses—"

"That one's okay, Harold."

"The other one is about the grizzly bear—*Lost Trails*—"

I got on my bus. "Six forty-two, Harold. I'll be ready."

He looked puzzled and walked away slowly getting wet.

I could see that we had the beginning of a problem. Harold the Hawk was being considerate of me, and I didn't know how to handle it. He was trying not to push me into a situation without giving me a choice. Not saying it had to be his way, this way or else.

But here I was, kind of old-fashioned, willing to accept whatever he wanted. I thought going to a movie wasn't that kind of big deal. Choosing one over the other wasn't that important. Being with Harold the Hawk was all that really was important to me. And of course I couldn't tell him that.

Maybe there would be another time, I thought, where something important might come up. Maybe then would be the time to find out for myself how I thought about something.

Meanwhile it was easier to go along with his idea, not making any waves. After all, he was the first boy to show interest in me. That seemed more important than anything.

When I got home, Chloris was ahead of me again. She was attacking a box of doughnuts with a glass of milk.

"What class did you cut this time?" I said.

"Teacher was sick. We got off early."

"Didn't you have lunch in school?"

"I couldn't eat. I was too mad at Patsy. My boss at the pizza joint, Mr. Perroni."

I helped myself to some of her doughnut. "You mean he turned you down on a raise?"

"I bought those doughnuts myself," she said. "Take it easy."

I put a nickel down on the table. "Here's five cents for two bites, cheapskate. So did he turn you down or not?"

She picked up the nickel and studied it. "Wait a sec. These cost a dollar for six. How do you figure five cents?"

I put a crumb of it down. "Okay, here's your change. Well, did he?"

She picked up the little crumb of doughnut and ate it. "Not only did that cheapskate turn me down, he told me business was so bad, he didn't think he could afford to keep all the girls working there."

I got a glass and poured some milk for myself. "Is it true? I mean is business really that bad?"

"How would I know? I only work there."

"Well, if you're not working as hard, you know it. Not taking as many orders, not carrying too many dishes, and so on. Going back and forth, you know."

"I don't count how many dishes I carry," she said. "If somebody is at one of my tables, I wait on them. There's usually somebody. Especially that pepperoni-pizza freak, he's always there."

"Wayne Gavin?"

"Well, I don't know any other pepperoni-pizza freaks, so it must be him."

"Have you learned how to get out of his car yet?" I said. "I mean, without having to kiss him good night?"

Chloris grinned. "I haven't been taking any more free rides with him, if that's what you mean. That doesn't mean I won't, if I feel like it. He's not too bad. And he must get a good allowance. I mean, I can always depend on him leaving a pretty good tip."

"What about the other girls there. Are they busy?"

"I don't know. Nobody's killing themselves, if you know what I mean. It's a crummy place anyway. People aren't standing in line and breaking the door down just to get in and eat some of Patsy's crummy pizza."

"Well, there's other restaurants," I said. "You can probably get a job at a lot of other places."

"I know, but Patsy's the closest to here. And anyway, none of the others pay any more. They all get you to work for practically nothing. You and your dumb ideas."

"It was your own idea," I said. "You heard me talking about getting more money for baby-sitting, and decided to try it yourself. Maybe you can go back to baby-sitting."

"No way," Chloris said firmly. "No more of that kiddie stuff for me. Working as a waitress is more fun."

"But you said—"

Chloris got up. "Oh, knock it off, Jen. I don't want to talk about it anymore. I'll probably get fired now for ever listening to you and your big ideas."

"Maybe you'll become a model some day and do TV commercials, and be rich and famous. Then Patsy will be sorry, I bet."

Chloris shrugged. "Yeah, well. That would teach him to pay his help a little more money, all right."

"Or you can open your own restaurant some day, and keep all the money yourself," I said. "You could call it Chloe's Cafe."

"You need money to open a restaurant, dumbbell," Chloris said. "Anyway, I wouldn't want to own a place where a lot of weirdos come in to eat."

"They've got to eat some place," I said.

"Well, not in my place. Let them find some other place," she said.

"Okay. So are you going back to work tonight?"

Chloris shrugged. "I don't know. I can't make up my mind. I need the money, so I guess I will. It's not that bad a job. In fact, I thought it was okay until you told me about asking for more money."

"I didn't tell you," I said. "You said you wanted more money like the thirty-five cents an hour I said my new price was, and I said maybe your boss Patsy might come up to twenty-five anyway. I also said what if he won't give it, remember?"

"I don't know why I listened to you in the first place. What do you know about anything?"

"I know I got another date with Harold the Hawk this Saturday," I said. "Another movie, he said."

Chloris stared. "That skateboard weirdo again? Why don't you go out with somebody normal?"

"He's all I got," I said. "I guess I don't know any normal people. Who do *you* know that's so normal?"

Chloris thought about it. Finally she shook her head. "Nobody, I guess. I'm the only one."

I remembered what happened at school and told Chloris about it. "Maybe you're not as normal as you think," I said. "There were at least three kids there who've had three divorces in their families. Nobody was hung up. They were laughing about it. This girl Ellen Kester said she had seven if we were allowed to count live-in boyfriends."

Chloris nearly gagged. "Seven? Her mother is weird."

"Well, you got to remember a lot of those are just temporary boyfriends, you know. They just stay for a while and then pick up and go. Those aren't real divorces."

Chloris clenched her jaws. "Well, she better not try any of that stuff around here. There better not be any of those cruddy live-in boyfriends staying here."

"Sarah Turnbull said it was fun. She said nobody stayed around long enough so she didn't get to miss them."

"Well, good for her," Chloris said, her eyes beginning to gleam now. "Tell that to your mother. Maybe she thinks she can pull that kind of stuff next."

"She's your mother, too. Anyway, what's the difference if she stays over at their place or they stay over here? If they're nice, I mean. If they're nice, they're not hurting anybody."

Chloris shook her head angrily. "Not here. They better not try that. This isn't a motel, you know. This is our home."

"Big deal," I said. "I bet if you asked around at your school, talked to some of your friends, you'd find a lot of this is going on now if their parents broke up. It can't be happening just to the kids in my class."

"I don't have to ask anybody," Chloris said through clenched teeth. "I don't care what anybody else does."

"Well, it's what's happening now. I guess it's Women's Lib. They're not hanging around crying now over spilt milk. They're beginning new lives, whatever they want to do. We got to get used to it. My friend Harold Osborne says his mom has had lots of different boyfriends since she and his dad got divorced. He's getting used to it, he told me."

Chloris tossed her hair angrily. "Well, that's his problem, not mine. Does she bring her boyfriends home for live-in dates, too, for weekends and like that?"

"He didn't say. I didn't get to ask him."

"What if she goes away with some guy for a weekend. I suppose that's okay, too, huh?"

"I don't know," I said. "What's the difference? Are we talking about Harold the Hawk's mother?"

Chloris got up looking very tired. "We better be."

27

Chloris decided to go to work that night. She left without having dinner, before Mom got home from her job. "I'll eat at Patsy's," she said. "As long as he's so cheap about money, he might as well feed me."

"If he's so cheap about money, maybe he won't like you to eat too much," I said.

Chloris tilted her nose up. "That's tough. It happens to be a law, Jen. He's got to feed the help. It can eat all it wants."

I had eaten once at Patsy's. The food really wasn't all that great. But the pizza and spaghetti were okay. Patsy had reasonable prices, too. It didn't cost an arm and a leg to eat there.

"Well, anyway," I said. "You need the job so you don't want to get fired. I don't think it's a law that Patsy's got to feed steak and lobster to the help."

"It's just his luck I don't feel too hungry tonight. A pizza is about all I feel like right now." She paused at the door. "I'll talk to you later. Don't go to sleep."

"I can't afford to sleep," I told her. "I got too much homework."

Chloris shrugged. "Well, I can always wake you up."

The door closed behind her and I got my books out of my desk. The telephone rang. I didn't recognize the voice.

"Is Chloris there?"

"She just left," I said. "Who's calling?"

There was silence at the other end. Then I heard him hang up. I wrote my memo on the pad for Chloris: *Some jerk called. Wouldn't leave his name. Must be your pepperoni freak. I could smell his breath.*

I got to my books again and then the door opened. It was Mom. I closed my book. It was going to be a rough night for homework.

I got up to meet her. "Did you have a good day?"

Mom's face looked pale and tired. She nodded mutely and stared a few seconds. "I don't know if it was a good day or not. I'm exhausted."

"Gy," I said. "How come? Did you have a lot of customers?"

Mom grimaced and sank back in the living-room chair without taking off her coat. "It's not that, so much. Since I've been promoted to my new job as buyer, I'm running around all day trying to keep things in order. That means checking on a lot of people, and believe me, Jenny, people can take an awful lot out of you." Her eyes shifted and she turned toward the bedroom. "Where's your sister?"

"She left for her job."

Mom glanced at her wristwatch. "This early?"

"She was going to have dinner there."

Mom stared at me mutely, then sighed. "There's something wrong with your sister. I wish I knew what it is."

"Oh, it's nothing," I said. "She was getting kind of jumpy hanging around. She's kind of worried about her job. She asked her boss Patsy for more money and he turned her down."

"She probably doesn't deserve more money," Mom said. "You know her. She doesn't put out. I'm afraid Chloris is going to grow up thinking the world owes her a living."

I waved my hands. "It's not that big a deal, Mom.

I told her I raised my baby-sitting rates thirty-five cents an hour. So she decided to ask for the same thing."

Mom looked petulant. "She could have asked me about it. I could have told her you don't get more money from your employer until you've proved that you're worth it."

"Well, anyway, it's no big deal. He didn't fire her or anything."

"That doesn't mean he won't," Mom said. "Do you realize how long I worked at Bontel's before they gave me this promotion I have and more money?" Her voice rose. "And don't think I don't work for it. Look how tired I am. I could just barely manage to get out of the car and walk upstairs."

"Maybe you're working too hard, and it ain't worth it," I said. "Maybe you'd be better off with your old job back."

Mom looked at me open-mouthed as if I'd gone crazy. "Go back to my old job? After working so hard to get this promotion? What do you think we live on—air? It takes a lot of money these days to run a single family with two growing girls."

"Maybe we could cut down," I said. "We don't eat that much. And Chloris can take all her meals at Patsy's."

Mom shook her head. "You don't understand, Jenny. You're too young to understand. The way money is today, it takes two working parents to support a family."

"Okay," I said, trying to sound cheerful and convincing. "So you'll get married again. Just pick a husband with a lot of money."

Mom waved her hand limply. "That's easier said than done. There aren't that many available husbands around willing to take on a woman with two teenage girls, you know."

"Okay," I said. "So we'll manage anyhow. I'll get

a good job soon, and if Chloe keeps her job, we'll put it all together and—"

Mom exploded suddenly, her voice rising almost to a shriek. "You don't know what you're talking about. It's not that easy." She began to cry, her voice turning harsh. "I've never found a decent man to support me, and now that I've finally found somebody I like, who really cares, you girls don't—" Her voice broke then and she buried her face in her hands. "You can't understand. What happens when you two grow up and I'm all alone?"

I didn't answer for a long moment. I felt sorry for Mom and hated to see her cry. Maybe a year ago I might have run to her, put my arm around to comfort her, help dry her tears. But when she said she hadn't found a decent man to support her, it wasn't true. I knew Fidel was decent. Maybe he didn't make too much money at being a sculptor and artist, but I remembered that money wasn't the reason Mom divorced him.

I stood stiffly feeling awkward. "Maybe you'll find somebody else before we grow up. You said yourself you meet a lot of different and interesting men on your job."

Mom shook her head, then got herself back into control. She took a tissue out of her bag and dried her eyes. "Well, that's true enough. At least some are interesting, not that I know them that well."

"You kind of liked that Mr. Sloan," I said. "What happned to him?"

"Nothing's happened to him," Mom said sharply. "He's divorced and has two teenage children himself. If we were to form a closer relationship, it would mean sharing a home at times with two other girls your age."

"How come? Don't they stay with his last wife?"

"Yes. But they're entitled to visit with their father."

I shrugged. "So it's no big deal. Maybe we'd like them."

"Maybe you would," Mom said. "I know your sister wouldn't. You know she wouldn't. You probably know her better than I do."

I remembered how Harold the Hawk felt about this problem with stepparents. "So what?" I said. "It's still your own life. My friend Harold the Hawk Osborne explained it to me. His mother has been dating a lot since she got divorced. And Harold says he found out he didn't like the idea of having a new stepparent until he watched a TV show about it. And that the kids worry about losing love from their own original parent."

Mom's face brightened. "Your friend said that?"

"He said he hated them at first. Now he goes along with whatever happens."

"He sounds like a very mature and intelligent boy. Is that the one who took you to the movie—the boy with the skateboard?"

"He asked me for another date for this Saturday. Is that okay?"

Mom shrugged. "I don't see why not. He certainly seems level-headed." She got up looking less tired. "I'm glad you told me that, Jenny. You've helped me make a rather difficult decision."

I was puzzled. "What about?"

She was moving away, heading toward the other room. "Excuse me, Jennifer, I have to make a phone call."

I went back to my room to pick up on my homework. Mom was dialing, and then I heard her say, "Hello, George. This is Marge. Guess what?" She closed her bedroom door then and that was all I heard. Then after a few seconds, I heard her laugh.

I looked down at my notebook page. I had doodled the name "George." I studied it for a while and then added the name "Sloan."

He was the good-looking man Chloris and I had

started to hate on sight. The one I had made Mom cry
about. It was good to hear her laughing now, talking
to the same man.

I thought of Chloris. Tough, I told myself, she'll
just have to get used to it. We're not babies. Mom's
got her own rights.

I hoped Mr. George Sloan would keep her laughing. Mom was a lot more fun when she was happy.

28

Mom's happy new mood got to me, making me
feel good all over, and I started writing my English
report for Mr. Culbertson. It was supposed to be
about skateboarding and Women's Lib. That was easy
because my attraction for Harold the Hawk was doing
strange liberating things to me inside. I mentioned
Women's Lib and how I felt about it, the rules they
had which didn't seem right for me just starting out in
a romantic relationship. And I remembered all the
things Harold the Hawk had told me about his mom
and the stepparent problem.

It all tied up with me, Mom and Chloris. I wrote
about what was happening, and what I wanted to
happen. That Mom would find a nice guy and fall in
love, that Chloris would accept that, and then we
could be one big happy family again. The guy she
was talking to now on the phone, George Sloan, might
be the one, but I didn't put down any names and left
it open, just in case.

I heard her voice through the wall. She was talking to Grandma Grace now. "But, Mother, you won't have to do anything. The girls can take care of themselves for a few days. I'd just like you to be there so they won't be alone."

I made a mental note. "Wow! It's happening!"

I thought about Mr. Sloan and his two daughters. It would be terrific if we liked each other. Then I could bring Kathy into it, and we could all be friends. I worried about Kathy being alone with no sister, just herself and her mother. And her thoughts turning in all the time about her size. I made another mental note to ask Mom if Mr. Sloan's kids were small or tall. If they were small, it would be good for my friend Kathy.

I wrote about new stepsisters in my report, about how nice that could be. Providing they weren't pains, I thought. What if they were like their father, and talked the same way Mr. Sloan did? That could be a problem, all right.

Would I be willing to accept Mr. Sloan and his daughters as they were? And then I had to consider what if Mom and Mr. Sloan didn't get married, but just had the new kind of relationship my friend Harold the Hawk had told me about.

I put down my pen. From Mom's conversation with her mother on the phone, she was planning something. Now I had to think of Chloris and how she would react to it. I could see that whatever happened now would depend upon how much Mom wanted her own life. In the new world of Women's Lib, you didn't have to be a mother all the time. You could be the person you were before, or wanted to be again.

If Mom decided to do her own thing, and ignore how Chloris felt about it, she would be taking a big risk. It would be her will against that of Chloris. Taurus the bull against Scorpio the schemer. It would be like a declaration of war for Mom to declare her own independence.

If Chloris had her own way, nothing would ever happen. We would stay at a dead end forever. I wished I could talk to her, get her to understand, but I knew it was hopeless. She was set into her own groove and intended to remain in it. She would never forget our dear dead daddy, and would always use his memory against Mom to keep her from living again.

I went to the bathroom.

"Telephone," Mom called, knocking at the door.

I opened the door. Mom was smiling. "For me? Who is it?"

"I didn't ask," Mom said. As I went past her, she said, "I'll be starting dinner. After you finish your call, you can set the table, Jenny."

I picked up the phone, nervously. "Hi. This is Jennifer Carpenter."

"Hi. This is Harold Osborne. Formerly the Hawk."

"Why 'formerly?' "

"Because I just fell out of a pool."

I laughed. "Harold, how can you fall out of a pool?"

"I got up and hit a vertical lip at speed, just sliding on the center of my board, no wheels touching, but before I could drop back in, I got airborne and nearly totaled a tree."

"Did you get hurt?" I wondered if this was going to be Harold's way of canceling our movie date.

"No. Only my board. Now I need to buy new trucks. Can we go Dutch on Saturday?"

"Sure," I said. "I'll have all that money from my baby-sitting job Friday."

"Good deal," Harold said. "Next time I'll spring for all of it. Right now I know I'm tapped out, or going to be."

"It's okay, Harold. You've done a lot for me, and I appreciate it."

He sounded surprised. "I have?"

"Yeah. You know. Telling me about your mom's dating, and how you went through it all."

"Is that where it's at over there?" he asked.

"Well, sort of," I said.

"It takes a while to get used to it," he said. "I mean, you can understand what's happening, and even why, but that doesn't mean you're going to like it."

"I think I'm going to like it, Harold," I said. "How long did it take you to get over it?"

He whistled. "Who said I ever got over it? It still bugs me when she goes out on a date with some new guy. But there's something worse, harder to take. That's weekends."

I tried to sound casual. "Why is that worse?"

"It's crazy," he said. "I just don't like my mother doing that. I know it's okay, understand, but I still don't like it. So don't give me any medals."

"Maybe this will help you understand, Harold. Being a mother has nothing to do with it. She was a girl before she became a mother, wasn't she? She can still be both, can't she? And what happens when you grow up and move away for your own life? Is she still supposed to be a mother and just hang out there?"

The phone was silent for a few moments, and I thought I had lost Harold. But he came on again, speaking very fast. "Hey, I never thought of that, and I should have. It's a very good point, you know."

"Well, yeah. I thought you understood all that."

"To tell you the truth, Jen, I thought I did, too. But I guess I didn't, when you come right down to it. I suppose it's some old moral code that got stuck in my head, and I wasn't able to get rid of it. Not totally, that is."

"Well, maybe it's easier for me to see the mother's side of it because I'm a girl, Harold."

"I don't know," he said. "We're supposed to see all sides of these things, Jen. I can see I still have some of the old masculine hang-ups, after all. I got to work on that."

"You're doing okay," I said. "So are we still all set on the movie date—six forty-two?"

"That's solid. Hey, did you mind that I didn't try to kiss you good night last time?"

I didn't know how to answer him, "Well, how did you feel about it, Harold?"

"I thought I should have. Only I didn't think of it because it was so weird going out on a date with a girl. Plus the fact that I was too chicken, of course."

"Well," I said, "maybe I was chicken, too."

"Terrific," he said. "Maybe we'll grow up together."

I hung up not daring to say another word.

29

I was asleep when Chloris got home. Mom had decided to go out to a movie with her mother and wasn't back yet. Chloris was whistling, moving things about. She seemed in a good mood.

"What happened?" I said. "Did you make a lot of money on tips tonight?"

She smiled. "Not bad. I didn't do bad at all."

"What's not bad? How much? As long as you woke me up, you might as well let me see the money."

She opened her purse and turned it upside down on my bed. There were several bills and a big pile of coins. "We were extra busy tonight, and I guess I gave extra good service because everybody was tipping me like mad."

"Including your pepperoni-pizza freak? Him, too?"

"Him, especially." Chloris began to dance dreamily around the room as she removed her blouse. "He turned out to be not such a freak, after all. I let him drive me home again tonight."

"I can tell," I said. "Your lipstick is all smeared."

"It is?" She leaned close to the mirror examining her lips. "Good thing Mom isn't home or I'd have to explain it. Where is she—working late again tonight on inventory?"

"She went to a movie with Grandma."

Chloris sniffed. "That's good. The less I see of her, the less we have to fight about."

I wasn't surprised to hear her say that. She and Mom were always at it, it seemed, a long-standing continuing battle of wills.

"Tell me more about Wayne Gavin, your pepperoni-pizza freak," I said. "How come you changed your mind and let him drive you home again? Last time he fogged your mind, remember? You said he wouldn't let you out of his car until you kissed him good night. And you forgot how to open a door handle and escape."

Chloris threw herself down on her bed looking up at the ceiling. "Well, he gave me a very good tip. A dollar for a two-fifty order. That showed he was interested in me, don't you see? And he keeps asking for a date every time he comes in. So I figured I might as well get to know him better before getting stuck on a date with him."

"So what do you know about him now that's worth a dollar?"

"He wants me to go up to Mammoth with him some weekend, you know. Skiing. I told you. Him and a bunch of other kids he knows."

"Mom would never let you do that."

Chloris nodded, still smiling. "I know. But it doesn't mean I still may not do it."

"Rotsa ruck," I said. "Anyway you don't know how to ski, and besides, what's so great about skiing?"

"I can learn, can't I? Wayne is a great skier, and says he'll teach me how. The other kids do it, so it must be fun."

"Is Wayne going to pay for you at the ski lodge, too?"

Chloris shrugged. "He didn't say, but he invited me, didn't he? Anyway, I have money of my own, you know. I've been working nights for a long time."

"Yeah, but I thought you were saving up for a car for when you go to college," I said.

Chloris turned over, kicking her legs in the air. "Maybe I won't go to college. Maybe I'll marry Wayne."

I stared. "Marry? You're not even sixteen yet."

"Big deal. So what? Anyway, I didn't say I was going to marry him tomorrow. But that's one of the reasons I want to go up to Mammoth skiing with him. So I can get to know him better."

"I guess you changed your mind about him being a pepperoni-pizza freak, huh."

Chloris smiled. "Sort of. He's very good-looking, you know. And he's crazy about me."

There was the sound of a key turning in the lock. Mom coming home. Chloris leaned toward me, her face contorted with a severe frown. "This was all between you and me, Jenny, understand? I'll tell her about it my own way."

"Big deal," I said.

I turned over and tried closing my eyes and falling asleep. It took a long time. I didn't like what was happening in my house. It was as if suddenly everything there was on very shaky ground, and at any moment the whole place might cave in. They have a lot of earthquakes in Southern California, but my family was making its own.

30

Chloris had already left for school Friday morning, and it was just Mom and me having breakfast when she dropped the first bombshell.

"I've decided to go away this weekend," she said. "I'm worn out. I can use the rest."

I was making my scrambled egg and toast. Although Mom's news was something I had been expecting, I still couldn't find the words to answer her. I kept on stirring my egg over the flame, thinking of this and that to say, feeling awfully hot and nervous. My egg was done before I was ready and I had to scrape it out of the pan.

"That's a good idea," I said finally. "When you leaving?"

"Early today after work." She pointed to her bag near the door. "Grandma will come over this afternoon to take care of you girls."

Grandma Grace and I got along fine. We always had things to talk about. "Well, okay," I said. "If she wants to. But we can manage. We're not babies."

"She doesn't mind," Mom said. "After all, she lives alone. She has nothing really to do."

I wanted to ask Mom if Mr. Sloan was going along but I didn't dare. Weekends, I remembered my friend Harold saying, were tough. "Where you going?" I said.

"Palm Springs. I'll be back Sunday evening."

My egg and toast wasn't going down too well. "Did you tell Chloris yet?"

Mom shook her head and drank her coffee. "I'll do that when I get home."

"Uh—she doesn't always come right back here after school," I said. "Sometimes she goes over to her friend Sue's house."

Mom smiled thinly and pointed to a piece of paper I hadn't noticed on the table. "I left her a note to come directly back after school."

"Well," I said, "I hope she got to read it."

Mom tossed her hair. "She couldn't miss it. I left it propped up against her cereal dish."

I remembered Chloris' own plan to go skiing up at Mammoth with her pepperoni-freak friend, and could guess how Mom would blow her stack at that idea. Knowing Chloris, I also knew what her reaction would be to Mom's going away for a weekend. One way or another, there was going to be a lot of noise around the apartment in the afternoon.

I couldn't tell Chloris' secret plan to Mom. And now Mom had a plan, too, but she wasn't telling it all like it was, I thought.

Was she taking off by herself? I know she hates to drive alone. Was she going with some other woman friend? Then why couldn't she tell me that?

The only other possibility I could think of was her going away with Mr. Sloan. I wanted to be able to tell Mom that if she was going away with him, it was okay with me. But I couldn't say that if she was keeping it a secret.

If she was going off with him, and cared enough for him to do that, then she should have been able to tell me that this was the way it was, the way it was going to be. That she would be doing her own thing. Leading her own life.

And then it would be up to Chloris and me to understand and accept her independence. I didn't want her to be wishy-washy or evasive about something so important to her.

I carried my plates to the sink to wash them off. "When are we going to meet Mr. Sloan's daughters?" I said, trying to sound casual, as if it had just occurred to me.

I felt her eyes on me but kept rinsing the dishes. "Sometime soon, I suppose," she said, after a while.

My school bus was due soon, and I couldn't keep washing those dumb plates forever. I put them on the drain to dry, put the milk and butter back in the refrigerator. "Well, I got to be shoving off," I said.

"Have a good day," Mom said.

"Yeah, you, too." I turned away not wanting her to see tears in my eyes.

31

I could see Harold the Hawk Osborne waiting for me the second I stepped off the school bus. That boy definitely had an effect upon me. My internal system went flipflop and things inside began to flutter. Weird, I thought, how can he do that to you?

He turned as I drew closer and I saw his right arm was folded inside a blue sling. There was a new patch across the bridge of his nose. He grinned at me and waved his other arm. "Hi," he said cheerfully. "In case you don't recognize the body, it's me."

I shook my head. "Harold, I think I would have more trouble recognizing you without any bandages at all. Did all this happen when you skateboarded out of that pool?"

He shrugged nonchalantly. "Yeah, well, those things are unpredictable. Sometimes when you try for a little extra, it works. Other times you're only carving out space with your body."

"That's terrible," I said.

"The tree is okay," he said. "Trees have total resistance to human contact. Not a mark on it."

"Well, you must have known the tree was there. You're very good at planning. How come you couldn't manage to fall out at another place?"

He nodded several times. "You're absolutely and totally right. That really is strange, when I think of it. I can plan outside events down to the most minute detail, I mean nonsporting events. But it seems that when I'm doing something in sports that's dangerous, my brain goes on vacation. You may not believe this but five-sixths of that pool area is completely free of hazards. I chose to fall out at the one point where that tree was."

"I believe it," I said. "Maybe you should give up skateboarding and pick a less dangerous sport, like climbing mountains."

He thought about it briefly before shaking his head negatively. "No, I think my genes are programmed for falling. If there was any way to fall off that mountain, I'd find it. What's happening over at your place?"

"Quite a lot," I said. "It's all gonna happen today, this weekend—everything. The Carpenter family is gonna explode in a million directions. And there's nothing I can do about it."

He whistled. The bell rang and we started walking together. "If you want to tell me about it, we have five minutes before classes."

There was always something about Harold the

Hawk that made me trust him absolutely. He seemed to be unnaturally honest, never hesitated to admit when he was wrong and didn't waste a single moment about telling me when I was right. It was as if he was a much older person, and I suppose that's what always gave me the confidence to tell him all. Either that, or I simply liked him so much that I couldn't bear to have any secrets that might keep us apart.

He bent his head, listening closely as we went along the long hallway. Kids were hurrying, some running, seemingly unconcerned about running right through us. But Harold the Hawk held me by the elbow close to his side, and didn't allow anybody to pass through us.

I told him first about Chloris intending to go up to Mammoth on a ski trip with her pepperoni-pizza friend freak, and Harold simply nodded, not interrupting, not offering any comment, not even one of surprise. The next part was more difficult, trying to explain about Mom.

"I'm not positive that she's going away with her friend, Mr. Sloan, but it's my guess. She hasn't mentioned anything at all about going with someone."

Harold shrugged. "If it's her first time for an outing like this, it's not very likely that she'd care to confide in you or your sister. Maybe later on, if it becomes a more frequent happening, and you get to know her friend better, she might let you in on it. Right now, you see, she couldn't afford to take a chance of letting anything spoil it."

"Is that how your mother did it, Harold?"

"She went away several times without bothering to explain it to me. Weekends. Holidays. Meanwhile, this guy kept coming over to our house. He wasn't too bad, and I got to know him better, even to like him a little. By the time she finally told me, I didn't need it. I already had guessed what was going on with them."

"What did you say then?"

He thought briefly. "Nothing much. I grunted something to the effect that it was okay. Something idiotic like that. Can you imagine what a dumb reaction that was?"

"What was?"

"Me having to tell her it was okay for her to do what she felt like doing."

I nodded. "Yeah. I know just what you mean."

We had reached the end of the hallway now, the point where we usually separate to go to our separate home classes. Harold shook his head and rumpled his hair, as we stopped. "I see your problem. You're worried that your mom won't let Chloris go away. And Chloris is going to dump it all about your mom going off. It will be a terrific hassle, all right."

"I know. What can I do about it, Harold?"

He shook his head regretfully a few times before speaking. "Not too much, unless you could get your sister to cool it, which apparently you can't. All you can do is hope for the best. A helpless situation. If Chloris doesn't take off, who's going to stay with you two girls?"

"My grandma. My mom's mother."

Harold the Hawk grinned suddenly. "Have you thought about how your grandmother is going to take it? Her own daughter?"

I admitted that no, I hadn't. I remembered Mom's voice wheedling at Grandma over the phone. "You must think I'm awfully dumb worrying about all this," I said helplessly.

"Hey, listen. I know what's happening with you inside. I went through the same process. It's a very insecure feeling. Total anxiety and helplessness. If it's dumb, maybe it's natural to be dumb about it."

I held my hand out to shake his. "Thanks a lot, Harold. You're really very nice to talk to."

He took my hand in his, and leaned forward suddenly. Before I realized it, he kissed me. It would

have been somewhere on my right cheek, but I drew
back and caught it on the nose instead. Harold the
Hawk didn't care. "You, too," he said.

I hurried to my class feeling better about everything. Except drawing back when he tried to kiss me,
I thought that was kind of dumb. But by the time I
got to my room and sat down, all the new good
feelings had suddenly evaporated. Liking Harold and
having him kiss me, even on the nose, still didn't do
anything about the big problem waiting at home.

All I could do was hope that by Saturday night
things would somehow have worked out to be better.
That it would be a happy home. And that when
Harold the Hawk took me out on our date, his aim
would be better when he tried to kiss me.

32

Grandma Grace has her own key to our apartment, and by the time I got home Friday afternoon,
she was there. Grandma and I are very fond of each
other, but this time I felt so nervous and unhappy
inside, I was almost annoyed that she was there. I
guess I didn't want her to be around when the big
storm broke. It was our personal problem, just Mom,
Chloris and me.

She had brought her overnight bag and was sitting watching TV. Grandma always used to tell me
how great books were to read, until she discovered
the TV soap operas. Since then, she's been hooked on

them. She follows all the daytime serials every day of the week.

I leaned over to kiss her cheek. "Hi, Grandma."

"Hello, pumpkin," she said, returning my kiss.

I must have been a fat baby. Or fat-faced. Why else would she call me pumpkin all my life?

She patted the sofa for me to sit near her, her eyes on the tube. "Betty just found out Dr. George, her husband, has been having an affair with his nurse Ellie."

I answered automatically with the one word I use to cover any situation. "Gy!"

Grandma nodded, watching the blond woman on the TV set cry. "But what's worse is Betty just found out she has an incurable cancer, and now she can't tell her husband because he'll think she's only trying to hold on to him."

"Maybe it's not incurable," I said. "Maybe she should try another doctor."

"I felt the same way," Grandma Grace said, "But the doctor who told her is Tom Goodwill, her old college sweetheart. He still loves her and wouldn't lie to her."

I set my school books on the floor. "Well, if he loves her that much, maybe he'll find a cure for her."

Grandma patted my hand. "You know, you and I should be writing these things, pumpkin. That's exactly what I thought. But I don't think Dr. George is going to leave Betty for his nurse anyway, because Ellie's not in such great shape herself."

"What's wrong with her?"

Grandma rubbed her side. "Liver problem. One of those extremely rare cases where nothing really can be done."

"Gy," I said.

"But she doesn't help matters any," Grandma Grace said sharply. "She's always drinking, trying to drown her troubles away, I suppose."

"Well, why doesn't Dr. George get her to stop drinking?"

It was a crazy conversation. I kept talking, wondering when Chloris was coming home. I could practically hear the time bomb ticking away.

Grandma Grace pointed to the TV set. It showed a young man walking down the street looking awfully depressed. He stopped in front of a bar, looked around and went inside.

"There's Ellie's old boyfriend," Grandma said. "She left him because he wouldn't stop drinking, and now she has the habit. Dr. George can't do anything about Ellie's habit because he thinks it's his fault since he won't divorce his wife Betty for Ellie."

I heard footsteps in the hall. A key turned in the lock and Chloris came in. She looked past me and at Grandma.

"Hi," she said. "What are you doing here, Grandma?"

"Just thought I'd pay you girls a visit," Grandma said. Chloris came over and kissed her cheek. "What's new with you?"

Chloris danced around. "I'm going to Mammoth this weekend. Skiing, you know."

Grandma laughed indulgently. "I haven't heard about that yet. I'd better wait until your mother comes home."

Chloris stopped dancing. "What's *she* got to do with it?"

Grandma patted the sofa. "Because she asked me to come over to stay with you girls because *she's* going away. Didn't she tell you?"

Chloris shook her head. Her lips parted but she didn't say anything. Her eyes gleamed at me, a questioning look. I shook my head in pantomine. *Who, me? No, I don't know a thing.*

"Why do you want to go to Mammoth?" Grandma said. "It's so cold."

"So what?" Chloris said. "It's fun. A lot of kids from my class are going."

I interrupted. "Grandma, didn't Mom tell you I'm baby-sitting tonight?"

Grandma blinked. "Well, no, she didn't. She mostly talked about wanting me to stay over here to keep you girls company. What time are you coming back?"

"Eleven or twelve," I said. "Sometimes Dr. and Mrs. Klugherz stay out a little longer on Friday night."

"Well, I can watch TV," Grandma said. "And Chloris can keep me company."

"I just told you," Chloris said loud and heatedly. "I'm going away."

The door opened and Mom came in. Chloris had been yelling and Mom must have heard her out in the hallway. "Going?" Mom said. "Where are you going?"

"Up to Mammoth," Chloris said, facing Mom firmly.

Mom ignored her, went over to her mother and kissed her on the cheek. "When did you get here, Mother?"

Grandma shrugged. "A little while ago." She shook her head. "You should have told me, you know. Things are kind of mixed up here. Jenny is baby-sitting, and Chloris is going skiing up at Mammoth."

Mom kept her cool and smiled. "Well, Jenny won't be very late, and Chloris and I haven't spoken at all about her going up to Mammoth. She isn't going, so there's nothing for you to worry about."

"I am, I am, too!" Chloris yelled.

Mom stared at her coldly. "Some time, perhaps. When you're a little older. But not this weekend, for sure. It so happens that I'm going away this weekend. That's why Grandma is staying here."

"Why?" Chloris yelled. "Where are you going?"

Mom shrugged. "Palm Springs. I've a chance to go away for a few days, and I'm going." She looked angrily at Chloris. "There's no way you can throw one of your tantrums and spoil my plans."

Chloris jumped up and down in silent fury, glaring at Mom. Her eyes filled with tears. She turned abruptly and ran to our bedroom. The door slammed. The apartment shook. Mom winced and made a move as if to go after Chloris but changed her mind. She leaned back on the sofa near Grandma and me, wagging her head. "I honestly don't know what I'm going to do about that girl. If I let her, she would do anything to spoil my life."

Grandma patted Mom's hand. "She only wanted to go with her friends. It must seem exciting to her. But she'll get over it. I can remember several times when you and I had differing opinions on when and where to go, too."

Mom was about to answer that when Chloris came storming out of our bedroom. She stopped squarely in front of Mom.

"Who are you going away with?"

Mom's face paled. "That's none of your business. I'm just going away for a few days. Period."

Chloris stood there, eyes blazing mad. "It *is* my business. You're probably going away with some guy, right?"

Mom looked at her. "That is still none of your business."

Chloris picked a magazine off the coffee table and slammed it down. "It is, too, my business. You can't do that!"

"Why not?" Mom said, swinging her crossed leg.

"Because you're a mother," Chloris yelled.

It sounded kind of corny to me, but Mom reacted to it. "I'm still a person, a human being," she shouted. "Who are you to tell me what I can or cannot do?"

"I'm your daughter," Chloris yelled. "That's who. And mothers don't go running off with guys to shack up over the weekend."

There was a long moment of shocked silence, and then Mom got up. I could guess what she was going to do, and I wasn't wrong. She grabbed Chloris and slapped her hard across the face. Chloris stood there stunned, an outraged expression on her face. She started to say something but Mom hit her again before she could say a word.

"Don't you ever say those words to me again," Mom said, her voice shrill and rising. "Don't you ever dare!"

Chloris swayed on her feet, both arms rigid, her hands clenched into fists. There were red marks on her cheeks where Mom had slapped her. She put her hand to her face, and then looked at it as if expecting to see blood.

"I hate you! I hate you!" she screamed. "You're never going to see me again."

She scooped up her windbreaker and rushed out the front door, slamming it behind her. I could hear her footsteps running down the hallway for a long time, and then I couldn't hear anything. Then there was a new strange wailing sound. I turned to look at Grandma and then Mom. It wasn't either of them. I heard more hysterical sounds and located them finally. They were coming from the tube, the TV set was still on. Betty the blond woman was having a crying fit over something.

"Oh, will you turn that stupid thing off!" Mom yelled.

I jumped, then looked at Grandma. She nodded to me, unruffled. "Betty always cries near the end," she said. "That woman has more problems than anybody."

"Not more than me, she hasn't," Mom said. "She doesn't have a foul-mouthed brat like I have." She looked at her wristwatch. "I've got to get ready."

She hurried toward her bedroom. I was at the TV set ready to turn it off, but not wanting to be rude to Grandma. She smiled.

"If you think Betty's having trouble now, wait till

tomorrow. She doesn't know yet that her husband just promised Ellie he was definitely going to see a laywer about his divorce."

"Gy," I said. I was worried, and not about Betty and her dumb problems on TV. "I hope Chloris didn't mean what she said."

"What was that?" Grandma said, reaching over and turning off the set.

"About leaving, and never coming back," I said.

Grandma smiled and rubbed her hands. "Oh, she didn't mean it. Children never mean those things."

"You don't know Chloris," I said.

Grandma laughed. "Children are all alike," she said. "Some days, there's no reasoning with them."

I wanted to tell her she was wrong. That Chloris wasn't the type who could forget things, just blow up and not mean anything, come back all smiles later. Chloris wasn't the type to forgive or forget.

But I didn't say anything because I was hoping she was right while I kept listening with one ear for a sound from outside that would mean Chloris had changed her mind.

Mom came out of her room wearing fresh make-up. She picked up her suitcase. She leaned over to kiss me, and began telling Grandma about what there was for dinner and so on, and she would be back late Sunday evening. Then she was gone and I realized I hadn't heard much of what she said.

I peeked out through the window curtain. There was a long black Lincoln Continental double-parked on our side street. A tall handsome man got out. Chloris and I had made fun of his extra polite manner after he took Mom out once. George Sloan. The one with two daughters near my age.

Mom came along with her weekend bag. Mr. Sloan took the bag from her with one hand, and drew her close with the other. Her arm went over his shoulder and he kissed her.

It wasn't a long passionate kiss, but I couldn't bear to watch it, and drew back letting the curtain fall in place. I had funny symptoms immediately.

1. My head hurt.
2. My stomach hurt.
3. I felt nauseous.
4. I was trembling.
5. My hands were sweating.
6. My knees felt weak and unsteady.
7. My pulse was pounding.
8. My neck hurt.

I realized those were a lot of symptoms over just one hug and kiss. I peeked out the window again. Mom was in the Lincoln Continental now, and it moved slowly away.

My heart continued to pound.

My thoughts flew to Fidel. How I loved him, how sorry I was to lose him. Why did she have to divorce him?

I was clenching my fists feeling betrayed. Feeling awful.

Then my good sensible Libra side came to the rescue.

What's with you? it asked.

I don't know. I feel terrible.

What's all this about feeling betrayed? it said. *What does that mean?*

Well, she kissed him . . . .

Good grief! my Libra side said. *I thought you were for her new life. Fidel is gone now, right? It's all over.*

I had to admit it was.

He's not coming back. That's past history, right?

Yeah, I guess.

So Mom is into her new life. You better get with it.

Okay, right on. What about all those crazy symptoms?

It sounds like you got the flu, my Libra side said.

33

Hanging around for some word from Chloris nearly made me late for my baby-sitting job. But she didn't call and I mentally called her a fink, and hurried over.

Dr. and Mrs. Klugherz were ready to leave. Their kids, Tara and Jeffery, were watching TV.

Mrs. Klugherz went through her usual routine with me, telling me what time the kids were supposed to go to bed. How I wasn't to give in no matter how they begged for more TV. That there were snacks in the fridge in case I got hungry, and so on.

I listened mechanically, nodding, hardly paying attention. My mind was still whirling around, wondering if Chloris had actually gone on the trip to Mammoth, or if this time her mind was made up and she was going to run away.

Mrs. Klugherz leaned closer. "You can expect us back by eleven-thirty, twelve at the latest. I left the number of the theater for you to call if anything goes wrong."

After they had gone, I played some games with the kids for a while, and then it was time for them to go to bed. They didn't argue about it, which made it a lot easier, and then I settled back on their big sofa and tried to relax. I realized that here it was my first night baby-sitting at my new increased rate, making a lot more money than I ever had before, and I couldn't even enjoy it.

There wasn't anything good on TV but I watched anyway hoping to get my mind off Chloris and Mom. After a while, I called our apartment to ask Grandma if Chloris had got home yet.

"No, she hasn't," Grandma said, "and I feel that's very rude of her, don't you? I mean, here I am making the big trip over to keep you girls company, and she waltzes out in one of her tantrums. Do you think that's right?"

"Well, no, Grandma," I said, "but she was all excited, you know. Chloe has been kind of nervous lately."

"I miss you, too, of course, but at least you have a job to do, baby-sitting."

"Chloris works, too, Grandma," I said. "That pizza joint."

"She's not there," Grandma said tartly. "I called."

"Gy," I said. "Then maybe she's gone to Mammoth Mountain, like she said."

"That's ridiculous, Jenny. She wouldn't go without your mother's permission, and she certainly wasn't wearing the warm clothing she would have needed to go up in snow country."

"Gy! That's right."

I remembered she had worn her old thin windbreaker when she rushed out, not the new heavier leather coat she had just bought.

"Anyway," Grandma said, "I'm very upset with her for doing something silly like this when I'm here. If she wants to fight with your mother, there are plenty of other times to do that when I'm not around."

"Don't worry, Grandma," I said. "Maybe she's hanging out with some of her friends. I'll call some of them."

"Well, call me back the moment you hear anything, pumpkin. I feel very foolish sitting here all by myself in your apartment. I have four walls and a TV set of my own over at my place if I wanted to be alone."

I didn't blame Grandma for being upset. It wasn't right for her to be alone when she had come over to help keep us company.

If Chloris wasn't at her job, she could have gone to a movie, or gone to visit some of her girlfriends, or really gone up to Mammoth with her pepperoni-pizza freak Wayne. I wished I knew more about Mammoth and ski country, and if this Wayne Gavin had really taken her there.

I got out the phone book and started to call some of the kids Chloris knew. The first two were out, and there was no answer. The third call was to Sue Brook, a close friend of hers. Sue's mother answered. Sue wasn't home, she said. I said I was Chloris' sister, looking for her. "I think Chloris is with Sue," Mrs. Brook said.

"Where's that?"

"They went skiing up at Mammoth," she said. Her voice sounded more surprised. "Doesn't your mother know?"

I said I didn't know for sure, that my mom had gone some place herself suddenly, and my grandmother was with us and didn't know if Chloris was coming home to dinner. And so on. A crazy answer because I couldn't think of what to say.

"Your mother must have known," Mrs. Brook said sternly. "The girls have been planning this trip for a long time. I can't imagine Chloris going without your mother's permission. Didn't she leave a number where she could be reached?"

I said maybe she had but I was somewhere else and the number was probably home where my grandma was, and so all we wanted to know was whether or not Chloris had really gone to Mammoth. No real emergency, I said. Just asking. My grandma wanted to know. And so on.

I'm really a terrible liar and once I start, I can't seem to get out of it. It gets worse and worse.

"Do you know who else is going?" I said.

"I know some of the boys, not all. Most of the girls. There were six, all told. They picked up Sue over an hour ago."

"Well, was Chloris with her, Mrs. Brook?"

"I didn't see her. A lot of girls were still in the car."

"Do you know who was driving?"

"I don't know the boy. I think his name was Gavin. Bobby or Richard."

"Wayne?" I said. My heart was pounding again.

"That's it," she said. "Wayne. I believe something was said about picking up some of the others on the way"

"And they already left?"

"I told you. Over an hour ago. It's a long drive up to there, you know. About five or six hours."

"Oh, yeah. Well, thanks."

"I suggest you tell your grandmother not to wait dinner for Chloris. I'm sure she went along. I believe Sue was expecting her to, anyway. She was going to get a special coat for it, as I recall."

"Yeah, well, thanks."

After hanging up, I wondered who to call next. Sue's mother seemed pretty sure, but she wasn't positive.

I looked up the number for Patsy's pizza joint. There were a lot of Patsy's pizza joints. Finally I found the right one.

A man answered. He didn't announce if he was Patsy or not. "How many in your party?" he said gruffly.

"I don't have a party. Is Chloris there?"

"Who?"

"Chloris. She's your waitress. Is she working tonight?"

"Who wants to know?"

"I'm her sister."

"So where is your sister tonight?" he said.

"I don't know," I said.

He muttered something angrily and hung up on me.

Before calling Grandma back and getting her still more excited and nervous, I called Harold the Hawk.

"Hey, I was just about to call you," he said, sounding very happy. "You at your baby-sitting job?"

"Yes. I've got a problem."

"Do you want me to come over so we can discuss it?"

"I think we better discuss this over the phone, Harold. It's about my sister. I think she's gone up to Mammoth with some of her friends. She had a fight with my mom and left."

"Well, that's up to your mother now, isn't it?"

I explained how it was about my mother. Harold whistled. I told him about calling Sue Brook's mother, giving him all the scoop. He whistled again.

"Do you know what make of car Wayne was driving?"

"No."

"Do you know where in Mammoth the group is staying?"

"No, I don't know that either. And I don't know for sure that Chloris is with them."

"Well, is she at her waitress job?"

"No, I just called there."

Harold whistled again.

"I wish you wouldn't whistle so much every time I tell you something, Harold. You're making me feel guilty, as if I did something wrong."

"Sorry," he said. "You're absolutely right. That's a terrible habit I have. It just means that I'm thinking, Jen. Nothing personal. I mean, you have nothing to feel guilty about. Tell you what, I'll call my mother about it, okay?"

"Isn't she there?"

Harold laughed. "Hey, it's Friday night. She's out on a date."

"Well, if she's out on a date, how do you know where to call her?"

"I'm talking about later on, Jen. She's probably out to dinner now with this guy, her boyfriend. Later, they'll go back to his place. She might stay there overnight."

I felt like whistling myself and was sorry I had criticized Harold about it. A whistle seemed to be the only way to respond to what he had said

"Maybe we ought to forget the whole thing, Harold. I didn't realize it was that complicated. I don't want to spoil your mom's date."

"That's okay. It only sounds complicated because you're still not used to the idea of your mother dating. Or living with some guy."

"You're right, Harold. Neither is Chloris and that's why everything is so screwed up now. She figured she had as much right to go away with some guy as Mom did."

Harold laughed. "Maybe she's got a point there. It sounds like something they should have discussed, so they would get their individual rights straightened out."

"I don't think my mom is ready to give Chloris any yet."

"Well, maybe you should call your mother anyway, if you think Chloris went on her trip."

"I don't know where she went, Harold."

"You said your grandmother is staying over with you. Perhaps she told her."

"I don't know. And even if we did know, it would spoil her weekend trip to tell her."

"Sure," Harold said. "I guess that's what your sister wanted."

"Maybe. This is too much for me now, Harold. I better hang up now, and thanks for talking to me."

"Hey, do we still have our date tomorrow night?"

"I suppose so, Harold. But you better check, just in case. I mean, if Chloris didn't go away, we can do it. Otherwise there's going to be too much excitement around my place. Mom would want me around. She'll be frantic."

"Yeah, I guess. But if you want to talk some more later, call me back."

"Okay. What are you doing?"

"Mopping the kitchen floor. I already did the bathroom."

I was so used to Chloris and me doing those chores, I never had thought about boys helping out, too. "How about the toilet bowl and wash basin, Harold?"

"Those, too," he said. "Don't forget you're talking to an only child. That means I'm the best cook, maid and housekeeper money can buy"

"You're nice, Harold," I said.

"Well, you don't get points for it, but it keeps everybody happy," he said.

34

Dr. and Mrs. Klugherz came home just a little after eleven-thirty. She was humming happily. "Did everything go all right, Jennifer?" I told her yes, and she opened her purse and took out her billfold. "Let's see. Your new rate is one thirty-five an hour?" I nodded yes. She began to figure it mentally and then shook her head. "That's too hard. We better make it one fifty."

I didn't say anything. Harold the Hawk was right.

She finally got a pencil and wrote the numbers down. "Comes to nine dollars. Is that right?"

I shrugged and said I guessed so.

She turned to her husband. "Do you have a ten-dollar bill, dear?"

Dr. Klugherz took out his money, a thick roll of bills. He extracted a ten-dollar bill and gave it to his wife. She passed it on to me. I looked at it.

"That's all right, Jennifer," she said, laughing. "Keep the change. It's only money."

Then Dr. Klugherz drove me home I folded the new bill in my pocket. Here I was rich and I couldn't enjoy it.

Grandma was in her housecoat, drinking coffee, watching TV. She looked at her watch. "It's nearly midnight. Did you get driven home?"

I nodded and showed her the ten-dollar bill. "Look at all the money I made."

Grandma's eyes widened. "For baby-sitting those few hours?"

"My rates went up, Grandma. Plus I got a little extra."

"Good for you," she said. She drew her housecoat around her tighter. "Did you find out anything about Chloris? She hasn't called yet. I'm beginning to get worried."

The telephone rang. I nearly broke my leg beating Grandma to it. "Chloris, where are you, you rotten fink?" I yelled.

"Hello. This is Sergeant Osborne," a voice said.

"Huh?"

"Sergeant Osborne. L.A.P.D." It sounded like a woman's voice. "Are you the party with a missing person?"

"Well, sort of," I said nervously. "Who is this again?"

"This is Harold's mother. The policewoman. Am I speaking to Jennifer Carpenter?"

"Oh, hi," I said. "Did Harold call you?"

She laughed. "No. I'm just taking time off so I can check out everybody in L.A. county to see who is missing."

Grandma was trying to attract my attention, making noises, gesturing. I shook my head at her, mouthing that it wasn't Chloris on the phone.

Hearing Harold the Hawk's mother's voice over the phone made me less nervous about her being a policewoman. She sounded nice and friendly. I liked her laugh, especially.

"Well," I said. "I hope Harold told you that my sister isn't really missing. I mean she's not here, and she's not at her job, but there are a lot of other places she could be."

"Such as?" Harold's mother said.

"She could be with some of her friends or she could be at a movie."

"What time did she leave?"

"A little after five."

"She'd be out of the movie by now," she said.

"Well, yeah. I guess."

"Does she usually stay up this late with her friends?"

"Well, no. She doesn't."

"Have you tried calling some of her friends?"

"Well, yeah. This mother of her best friend, Sue Brook, said she thought Chloris went along with her daughter to Mammoth."

"She thought? She wasn't positive?"

"No. She said she didn't see her. She only thought my sister went because they were talking about it. But there was kind of a big scene here. Between Chloris and my mom—so I don't know—"

"Have you contacted your mother?"

"No. Not yet."

"Do you know her present whereabouts?"

"Not exactly. I think Palm Springs someplace."

"I understand your grandmother is staying with you. Does she know where your mother is?"

"I'm not sure. Hold on, I'll ask."

"Ask what?" Grandma said.

"Where Mom is staying?"

"Who wants to know?"

"The police."

Grandma looked horrified. "The what?"

I waved my free hand. "It's okay. She's my friend's mother."

"Who is?" Grandma said.

"This lady on the phone. She's a policewoman."

Grandma toyed with her hair. "I don't believe I'm getting all this."

I pointed to the phone. "She's his mother. My boyfriend Harold. She's in the Los Angeles Police Department. She's calling to find out if she can help in case Chloris is missing."

Grandma looked around pointedly. "She isn't around, is she?"

I shook my head.

"She's missing, if you ask me," Grandma said.

For the first time I could remember, I got impatient with Grandma. I held the phone up. "She wants to know where Mom is in Palm Springs. Do you know?"

Grandma was shaking her head fretfully. "I don't know what good that would do. I don't like this a bit. Your mother asked me to keep you girls company over the weekend. She didn't say anything about the roof falling in."

I brought the phone closer. "Grandma doesn't feel like saying right now. Is that okay, Mrs. Osborne?"

"Sergeant Osborne," she corrected. "Well, I can understand how she feels about it. There's no point to pushing the panic button just yet. Would you happen to know where in Mammoth your sister might have gone?"

"No."

"Do you know who was driving the car?"

"Wayne Gavin. He's her friend. A senior at Emerson High."

"Make and model of the car?" she said.

"Huh?"

"Do you know what kind of car he drives?"

"No." I was getting frightened again. "A lot of other kids are supposed to have gone along, you know. Six, Mrs. Brook said. I mean, my sister isn't alone with him. Like that."

"I'll give you my work number to write down, Jennifer. If your sister comes home tonight, forget it. Otherwise, get in touch with me tomorrow morning." She gave me the number and I wrote it down with a shaking hand. "Just ask for Sergeant Osborne," she said.

"Okay. Thanks a lot."

"Don't mention it. How old is your sister?"

"Sixteen—well, nearly."

"What do you think of my son?"

"Harold? Well, he's okay. I mean he's nice."

"I think he is, too," she said. "Do you think that I'm overprotecting him?"

"Well," I said.

"I get it," she said, laughing. "I'll try to cut the strings a little."

"Harold's okay. He really is," I said.

"You sound okay, too. Have a good time at the movie."

"Well, that kind of depends on my sister, you know."

"If you need me, I'll do all I can, Jennifer."

Grandma looked intently at me when I hung up. "Is she—was the woman you were talking to really a policewoman?"

"You better believe it. She's a sergeant with the L.A.P.D."

Grandma fanned herself with a magazine. "I'm getting too old for these shenanigans. Bringing up your mother and my other two children took it all out of me."

"Took what out of you, Grandma?"

"Patience," Grandma said. "Also I was married over forty years. That's a lot of wear and tear on the human system."

"I don't know how you did it," I said. "I'm a nervous wreck already. In just one night."

"That's how it goes," Grandma said.

35

I got undressed and into my own housecoat, and sat with Grandma on the sofa watching TV. There was a late movie on about a vampire.

"Why do they still dress that way?" Grandma said.

At one of the commercial breaks, a newscaster came on. The High Sierras were expecting to be hit by a blizzard. A cold front was moving up on June Lake and Mammoth Mountain. Icy road conditions were expected. Travelers were urged to bring along snow chains. Also shovels to dig themselves out if the expected snowfall came.

I wrung my hands. "The dope—she'll freeze."

Grandma patted my hand. "Perhaps they'll hear

the weather report on their car radio and turn back."

The TV announcer was out of the bad news on the weather and into sports now. The Dodgers won. The Reds won. The Angels won. Nolan Ryan struck out fifteen batters.

"Do you think we ought to go to a baseball game someday?" Grandma asked.

I shrugged. "I didn't know you liked baseball that much."

"Well, actually I don't," Grandma said.

The telephone rang. I answered it trying not to guess. It was Mom. She asked if Chloris was back yet. I shook my head. I was nearly crying. "No, not yet," I managed to say.

"Did you try any of her friends?" Mom said.

I told her. There was a moment of silence.

"Sue Brook's mother said Chloris was going, too?"

"Well, she didn't see her in the car. Sue went and there were still some others to be picked up. So we're still not sure anyway."

"I just heard the news bulletin," Mom said. "They're expecting one of their worst blizzards ever up there."

"Well, yeah," I said. "But we're still not sure—"

Mom's voice was high, angry. "That rotten child! Did she tell you she was going?"

"Not exactly. She only said she felt like going, that she wanted to go. Sometime. She said sometime, not this particular time."

Mom mumbled something I couldn't hear. It was as if she was talking to somebody else, and then I realized, of course, her guy was with her, that Mr. Sloan. "Well, I'll have to call you back, I suppose."

"Are you in a hotel?" I asked.

"Yes, of course," Mom said. "A hotel, a motel. What's the difference?"

"I just meant do you want to leave the number, in case."

"What?"

"I mean in case you want to be notified."

Mom's voice became more nasal and nasty. "Notified of what? She's not home with you, is she? She told me she was going, didnt she? So I've already been notified, haven't I?"

I didn't like Mom too much when she acted like a crybaby. "Right on," I said. "Good night. Are you having a good time?"

Her voice rose. "How can I have a good time now? She did this on purpose. She planned it. You know what she's like, your sister."

"Yeah, well," I said.

"Let me talk to Grandma."

I handed the phone to her mother. "Mom wants to talk to you."

Grandma didn't wait for Mom to say anything. She went right at it with what she had to say. "This is the last time, Marge, believe me. You should have told me what was going on here. I haven't had a moment's peace. You asked me to step right into a hornet's nest—"

I could hear Mom's voice yelling and crying through the ear filter part of the phone. Grandma held the phone farther away from her ear until Mom's voice ran down, and then it was her turn again.

"Well, if you want my opinion, I'd say no, you should not have gone—"

Mom interrupted yelling again. Grandma listened, not looking entirely pleased or impressed.

"Well, maybe you didn't," Grandma said. "But the fact is, you're there in Palm Springs and I'm here with all that's going on—"

She waited for a while to give Mom a chance.

Grandma took her turn. "Somebody called from the police department—yes, that's what I said. A friend of Jenny's. They asked if we could reach you at a number there. No, I don't know what that's all about. I don't know what anything is about. I don't even know why I'm here."

Mom got in a few words.

Grandma listened with set lips. "I have no opinion about any of this at all, Marge. She's your daughter. You do what you think best."

There wasn't any interruption and she hung up. Then she reached over and patted my hand. "How about eating something, pumpkin? Would you like me to make you anything?"

I stared at her.

"Some eggs or a sandwich." She smiled at me. "Now don't worry. I'm sure that Chloris is all right, wherever she is."

I began to cry.

36

Grandma and I must have dozed off watching TV. The sound of a key turning in the lock woke me. Before I could get to the door, it opened. I was surprised to see Mom.

She looked around. "Is she here yet? Have you heard from her?"

I shook my head, no.

Mom closed the door and put her bag down as if it weighed a ton. She looked over at Grandma sleeping on the sofa, and shook her head.

"You didn't have to come all the way back," I said. "You spoiled your whole weekend."

"I know," Mom said wearily. "It couldn't be helped. Maybe there'll be another sometime."

Grandma woke up. She looked at Mom and then at her watch. "It's nearly three in the morning. When did you get here, Marge?"

"I just walked in," Mom said. "I'm really sorry I let you in for all this, Mother. I honestly never expected Chloris to do this. I thought she was bluffing."

"Well, I'm glad you decided to come back," Grandma said. "I'm a nervous wreck and I've got a terrible headache. If you'll excuse me, I'll go to bed."

"You should have gone to bed anyway," Mom said. "And not let Chloris ruin your night's sleep."

Grandma got up and tottered across the room. "I don't think I had much choice in the matter," she grumbled.

Mom helped her get set in her bedroom, and then came back and unpacked some of her things. Then she made some coffee and sat down next to me on the sofa. "Aren't you sleepy?"

I shrugged. "I dozed off a little. Anyway, I'm too nervous to be sleepy."

"Same here," Mom said. "What was that about your friend Harold's mother calling here?"

I explained it and found myself laughing. "She kept saying she was Sergeant Osborne, and I didn't get it, at first." I showed Mom the phone number Harold's mother had given me. "She said you could reach her here at her working number if you're still worried about Chloris being missing."

Mom stared dully at the number. "You mean she was still working that late?"

"No. That's for tomorrow morning. She called from her boyfriend's place. Or wherever they were staying on their Friday night date."

Mom frowned and put her cup down. "You're not supposed to say things like that. What's come over you?"

"It's okay," I said. "I'm not making it up. My

friend Harold told me about his mom dating. He's used to it, he told me, and doesn't mind anymore. His mom's been divorced a long time and it took him a long time to get used to it, he said. Especially going away for weekends with a guy. You know, like—"

Mom stared at me, open-mouthed. Her eyes were red, and I could tell now she had been crying. She wagged her head. "I never—" she said and stopped, reddening.

I wanted to be able to talk to her about my seeing her go off with Mr. Sloan in his Lincoln Continental, but then it would have meant I was spying on her.

"Anyway," I said, "after hearing my friend Harold talk about how he was adjusted to it now, I figured we could do the same here. I mean me and Chloris. In fact, we spoke about it a couple of times. Your dating, I mean. Even more than that actually—we talked about everything. You know, like unmarrieds living together. Like you and—well—anyway, all that stuff."

Mom stared. "You and Chloris talked about that?"

"Sure. Why not? It's what's happening, isn't it? I mean, even if it hasn't, it's going to, right?"

Mom shook her head. She was speechless for a long while, and kept toying with the long ends of her hair. They were damp now and curling. Finally, she pushed her coffee cup away and reached for the cigarette box on the table, set there for guests and Grandma who smokes.

"I thought you don't smoke," I said.

"I haven't since college." She lighted up, inhaled and immediately went into a coughing spasm. She put the cigarette down. "I guess I've got to get used to that again, too."

"I don't get it," I said. "If you don't like it—"

"I'm just trying it again now when my nerves are so frazzled," Mom said. "I expected to have a wonderful weekend at Palm Springs. But I couldn't enjoy it while worrying about Chloris. Not knowing what she

might really do. Now it appears she's done what she
wanted to anyway, and I've left my big date high and
dry. George—Mr. Sloan—was looking forward to us
being together, too." She looked steadily and openly
at me now. "We've been looking forward to it for
quite some time."

"Was he mad about taking you home?"

Mom smiled ruefully. "Disappointed, I'd say,
would be more like it. And I feel the same way."

I remembered her hugging and kissing him before she got into his car. "Do you love him?"

Mom picked up her cigarette again and watched
the smoke swirl upward. "I'm not exactly sure yet—
but I think so. It's a different feeling about being in
love than I'm used to. Not the way I had loved your
father. Not like with Fidel."

I didn't say anything. My throat began to hurt.

"I guess I've made mistakes. I didn't know what I
wanted, what I was looking for. I'm not so sure that I
know even now. That's what makes it so difficult with
George Sloan. But I think he understands. He's had his
divorce problems, too."

"How come you divorced them both if you loved
them? I don't get it," I said.

"I had personal reasons, which I don't expect you
to understand yet," she said. "I don't see any reason for
going into them now with you."

Okay, I thought, suit yourself. Up to now we
seemed to be having a nice mother-and-daughter conversation.

Mom glanced at me, took another drag from the
cigarette and put it down, waving the smoke away. "I
suppose you still hate me for divorcing Fidel."

I was surprised to find myself thinking of a fair
answer. "No, I don't think so. Not anymore. When
you first did it, sure. You knew he was like my real
father to me."

Mom nodded. "Well, it was something I had to
do at that time. I can't explain it. Don't think it's been

that easy for me without Fidel. I found out I loved him more than I realized at the time."

Yeah. A lot of good that does now, I thought, it's too late now.

Mom sighed. "I didn't have to hear it from you and your friend. I know nearly everybody seems to be breaking up. Singles living together. Maybe it's a disease going around. Perhaps we all need to get our heads examined. I don't know. We don't seem to appreciate what we have until we don't have it any longer."

I looked at her, then away, disappointed. I wasn't satisfied with her answers. I didn't hate her now for what she did, but neither could I reach out and pat her on the back and say, it's okay, so what, it didn't work out, so what.

"I don't get it," I said. "How can you get divorced from somebody you loved enough to marry?"

Mom twisted her hands. "I think there's something about being married and owning each other that changes things. Because sooner or later, things change and it's not the same. So you're unhappy, and he's unhappy, and you think who needs this, there must be a better way to live your life.

"You look around and see all those other people out there in the world. And so you make your move to be free. Only you're not really free because you're tied up still to all those other past memories and relationships. And by the time you get your head together, suddenly there aren't that many people out there in the world waiting for you. Sometimes you feel as if there's nobody left out there at all."

"Gy," I said.

"I mean," Mom said darkly, "you don't get that many chances."

"Grandma didn't get divorced at all. How come?"

Mom's eyes flashed, looking hurt and angry. "How do I know? We're different people. The times are different. They used to fight a lot when I was young, but she and Dad always were able to make it up somehow. I never was able to do that."

"Okay. So now you're beginning to date again. Maybe this time it will work for you."

"I can't manage dating a lot of different men, as some women do. And it's not too easy with two teenage girls. Not every man wants to be burdened with children again, especially ones that aren't his."

"What's the difference, if he loves you?" I said. "Anyway you said Mr. Sloan has two kids of his own. So he's got the same problem, right?"

"Maybe he's got a problem, but I don't know if it's the same problem, Jenny. You remember how your sister acted with Fidel. She wouldn't talk to him, give him the time of day, never acknowledged him as my husband. What makes you think she'd be any different with Mr. Sloan or any other man I wanted to marry?"

"So what do you care, if you love him?"

Mom twisted her fingers nervously. "I don't know. I can't stand that kind of friction. And I don't think I know what love means anymore. It seems from the time we're born, women are programmed to make ourselves attractive to men. To want them for husbands. To settle down with them and raise a family, and be happy forever and ever. Well, it just doesn't work out that way. Hardly ever."

"You mean Grandma wanted you to get married?"

"Grandma, Grandpa—it's the way we were all brought up then. All my friends. It's different today. Girls aren't falling into that trap now. They're trying other experiences besides getting married right off the bat."

"You mean living with a guy?"

Mom looked at me as if noticing for the first time that I wasn't her little baby anymore. Her lips trembled and her eyes moistened. "How did we ever get into this conversation? Why are you asking me all these silly questions?"

My temper flared. "What's silly about it? I got a boyfriend already, you know. Harold the Hawk. I like him a lot. He's very nice and fun to be with."

Mom smiled. "Okay. So you've got your first crush. It doesn't mean you have to marry him, Jenny."

"I don't *feel* like marrying him," I said. "All I know is I like him a lot. That's how it is right now. We got another date for tomorrow night. He's taking me to another movie." I looked at my watch. "I mean, if everything turns out okay with Chloris."

Mom bit her lip as she looked at her own watch. She drew her legs up on the sofa and began to cry.

"I don't know what's so terrible about that trip," I said. "She's not out with this guy all by herself. There's a whole bunch of them, you know. A lot of her other friends besides Sue Brook. Their moms must have said it was okay to go."

Mom nodded as if she heard me, still sobbing. Her voice was muffled coming from between her arms. "I don't know," she wailed. "I don't know. I might have given her permission some other time. But this was my chance to go away, and she took advantage of it. She ruined my weekend vacation. She's a mean, rotten child."

I shrugged. "Okay. So why are you crying about her?"

Mom straightened up suddenly. She looked cold and determined. "You're right. She doesn't deserve it." She moved her hand over the magazines on the table. "Where's that police sergeant's number? I'm going to call and have her declared missing. She's not going to get away with this."

I thought about Chloris being chased by police cars. It was like a TV movie in my mind. Searchlights, sirens, a police helicopter hovering over the car of that dopey pizza-pepperoni freak Wayne Gavin. Wayne was driving like mad on one of those snowy roads going up to Mammoth Mountain. The police helicopter was making him nervous. He was driving too fast. The kids in the car were cold, worried.

The road was narrow. There was a big drop to the valley below, hundreds of feet. Snow-covered rocks down there. Around the turn came a big bus. Wayne didn't have any room. The bus forced him to go outside too far. His tires skidded on the snow-covered icy road.

Chloris screamed. The car flew over the edge.

I was on my feet yelling. "Don't do it! Let her alone!"

Mom stared at me. She looked down at the scrap of paper with the number I had written. Her lips were set and I knew from her expression I couldn't budge her. She brought the telephone closer.

"It's none of your business," Mom said. "She's my daughter, and she's got to learn some things right now."

She began to dial.

I ran over and knocked the phone off the table. It made an awful crash. Mom looked at me with wide shocked eyes. "What's wrong with you? Pick up that phone and put it back on the table here."

"I won't! She's my sister! If you call the police, I'm going to run away, too!"

Mom jumped to her feet to face me. Her arm lifted and her hands jerked. I guess she was trying hard not to smack me. She hadn't done it too much in my life. She saved most of that for Chloris.

But then I never gave her that much of an opportunity. I was always the good one. *Goody Two-Shoes.*

Chloris was the rebel. The bad one.

The one who shouted and spoke her mind.

The one who always got punished.

I couldn't believe what was happening. Me and Mom standing face to face, yelling at each other.

Grandma came out of her room wearing a bathrobe. "What on earth is going on?" she said sleepily. "Don't you people know how to speak quietly?"

I was shaking, mad and frightened, knowing I had gone too far suddenly. Teaming myself up with Chloris at the worst possible time. Yet something inside wouldn't let me chicken out of it. It kept me standing up there to Mom, not knowing what was going to happen, and for the first time I could remember not caring.

"It's the same thing," I was yelling. "If you had a right to go away, so did Chloris. You both wanted a good time. So what's the difference? How come it was okay for you and not for her?"

Mom gaped at me, white-faced, unable to say a word.

Grandma Grace came over to me, making soft soothing sounds. She held and patted me. "Now, pumpkin, don't get excited and lose your temper. Everything will be all right." She hugged me very close and spoke over my shoulder to Mom. "Can't you see she's upset and worried sick about her sister? I'm really surprised at you, Marge."

Mom shook her head as if not believing any of this. She pushed back her hair, moving her lips silently. I'd never seen her look so furious as she did now. She picked up the phone again, her lip set in an obstinate line, and dialed.

"Operator, will you get me the police, please?"

I tried to struggle free of Grandma's arms, but she held me tighter. She stroked my hair and spoke soothingly. "It's all right, pumpkin, it's all right. She's only doing what she feels must be done, don't you see? She's worried, too."

Mom was speaking into the phone, her voice cool and emphatic. "I want to report a missing person—my

daughter. Her name is Chloris Carpenter. All right,
I'll spell it . . . yes, this is Mrs. Carpenter speaking.
Yes, I'll wait."

She waited a while and then began again. "Hello,
yes, my daughter has not returned home after an argument. She's been missing several hours. . . . Is it an
emergency? I don't know. She's gone without my permission up to Mammoth Mountain with a group of
friends, skiing. She's almost sixteen. . . . . What? a runaway, yes. I'd like her apprehended and brought
back, yes. . . ."

I never heard the key turn in the lock, being held
so close by Grandma. But Mom said, "Just a moment.
She just came in. Excuse this call."

"What?" Grandma said. She dropped her arms
from me and turned toward the door.

I stood there shaking, crying, unable to stop.

Chloris closed the door quietly behind her and
leaned back against it. Her face was very pale, her hair
windblown. She looked exhausted. Her green eyes
flicked to Mom warily.

"Well, I'm back," she said casually.

Mom was putting the phone down, having trouble putting it on its cradle straight.

I looked at Chloris. Her eyes met mine with
no expression. "I hate you!" I screamed. "I hate you,
hate you!"

Chloris stared back at me, standing limp against
the door. "So what else is new?" she murmured.

Something inside me exploded. There was a new
roaring sound inside my head. I rushed over to
Chloris, and began hitting her. She just stood there
making no move to protect herself. Not making a
sound. Grandma grabbed my arm and pulled me
away.

Chloris stood swaying. There was blood on her
lip where I had hit her. Red marks on her face. Her
green eyes gleamed.

"You're weird," she said.

37

Mom recovered her cool. "You look as if you haven't eaten," she said to Chloris. "I'll fix something."

"I'll do it," Grandma said, turning for the kitchen.

"No, Mother," Mom said firmly. "I'll do it. Go back to bed and finish your night's sleep."

Grandma lifted her arms. "Who can sleep around here with all that's going on?"

Mom was busy getting things out of the fridge and bread box. "Well, I'm sorry, Mother," Mom said. "I haven't slept either, you know."

"You're younger," Grandma said. "And anyway she's your child. But at least she's back safely, and that's the main thing."

"Yes, Mother," Mom said. "Do you want some scrambled eggs?"

Grandma yawned. "No thanks, I'm turning in." She went over to Chloris. "Are you all right?" Chloris nodded. "That's good, dear. Well, good night. We'll talk about it in the morning."

She leaned over to kiss Chloris on the cheek. Chloris stood there rigidly, not responding. "Your lip is bleeding," Grandma said. She sighed loudly and headed for Mom's bedroom.

Chloris put the back of her hand to her lip and stared at the smear of blood. She shook her head.

"Yeah. That's some weird sister I've got, all right." She walked toward the bathroom.

"Why didn't you stay away?" I yelled. "All that big talk about going, and here you are."

Chloris ignored me, walking right by.

"I guess you thought we couldn't live without you. That we'd be worried or something."

Mom came out of the kitchen with the mixing bowl, stirring some milk and eggs. "Knock it off, Jenny." She held up the bowl. "Do you want something to eat, too?"

"No," I yelled. "I'm going to bed." And I stormed into my bedroom and slammed the door behind me. I didn't want to hear any of the jazz about her skiing trip and why she didn't make it. My stomach hurt. I guess I was hungry at that and could have eaten, but I was still too mad. I undressed and went to bed. Then I realized I hadn't brushed my teeth. But Chloris was in the bathroom and I figured the heck with it.

I was still upset and shaking and couldn't fall asleep. I didn't understand why I was so angry when all I really wanted was for Chloris to be home safely.

I cried some more and got angry with myself for crying. She's not worth it, I told myself. She does whatever she feels like doing, and you're left out on a limb.

Next time it will be different, I told myself, just watch and see. Next time I'm not sitting home waiting and worrying over her. Next time I'm going out to a movie or something.

Then I began wondering about what really happened to bring Chloris back. I also wondered what was going to happen between her and Mom.

I sat up straining my ears, trying hard to listen. But with the darn door shut, I couldn't hear a thing.

Don't be dumb, I told myself. This is a family fight but it concerns you, too. You ought to be out there with them hearing what's going on. For all you know, it could happen again, and you would never even know how *this* one turned out.

I got my feet out on the side of the bed, and hesitated. Maybe it would be better for Mom and Chloris to be alone in this fight, I told myself. It's between those two now.

Like heck it is, I thought suddenly. I worried myself sick about it all night. It's my business, too.

I got out of bed fast and into my bathrobe again.

Chloris was just coming out of the bathroom. She kept walking toward the kitchen as if she hadn't noticed me.

"I decided to hear what happened," I said. "I need a few laughs before I go back to sleep."

Chloris ignored me.

Mom had set two places at the table for Chloris and herself. Chloris took her seat quietly. Not sullen, I noticed, just quiet. As if she had come to a great decision and was very relaxed with herself.

Mom turned from the range and saw me. "I decided I'm hungry, after all," I said. "What are you making?"

Mom pushed her hair back. "Eggs. Or I can make you some French toast, if you like."

"Eggs are okay," I said. I went to the fridge and took out the milk. I filled my glass, got a napkin, and set a place for myself at the table. Chloris still didn't say anything. I put the milk container back in the fridge. Mom added more eggs to the bowl.

"I'm glad you decided to join us, Jennifer," Mom said. "I think this concerns you, too."

I picked up my glass and sipped some of the milk. It was very cold. "Right on," I said. "I thought so, too."

Mom got the stirred eggs going in the big fry pan. The coffee she was making for herself began perking and she shut it off. It had a good smell.

She came over with the pan and pushed equal parts of the scrambled eggs on to our plates. She got the toast out of the toaster and brought that over, too, with jam and butter. Then she poured her own cup of coffee and sat down.

"Let's eat first," she said, "and then we'll talk about it."

She looked nervous and flushed. Without a glance at Chloris or me, she began eating.

Chloris sat looking at her plate. I decided now that this new quiet look she had wasn't relaxed, as I had thought. Her milk glass was empty, and I know she likes milk as much as I do. She hadn't said a word when I filled my glass and then took the container back to the fridge.

She was stunned, I thought. Or utterly exhausted. Maybe all she had gone through was more than I could imagine. I got up and brought the milk container back out of the fridge and set it down between us. Then I got busy with my eggs and toast.

Her eyes flicked to mine, surprised. "Oh, thanks," she said. She poured her glass full and then still holding the container began to drink greedily. She drank nearly all of it before setting it down. "That's good milk," she said, without expression.

"The eggs are good, too," I said.

"Oh," she said, and picked up her fork. Her first bite was tentative, and then she didn't stop putting stuff in her mouth until the plate was empty.

Mom had finished hers, too. She looked at my plate and Chloris'. "Maybe I should make some more," she said.

I finished mine to keep up with the family wolf pack. "Not for me," I said. "I'll just take some more milk."

Mom turned to Chloris. "Chloris?"

Chloris started to say something. She shook her head, silently. Her lips moved again soundlessly. Then her eyes filled with tears. She pushed her plate away. "I'm sorry," she said.

I watched amazed as she began to cry. I couldn't

remember Chloris crying ever at the beginning of an argument. As a rule, she got so excited about what she was hollering about, usually with Mom, that she wound up in tears. But she wasn't hollering now, simply sitting there, her shoulders shaking, crying, now burying her face in her folded arms.

Mom's eyes filled with tears and now she was crying, too. Her hand reached across to touch Chloris on the shoulder. "I'm sorry, too, Chloris," she said.

Chloris reacted to her touch as if she had been burned. She twisted back in her chair, recoiling from Mom's hand, leaving it dangling there in space. "Don't touch me," Chloris yelled. "You hit me before. If you hadn't hit me, maybe I wouldn't have gone."

Mom stood up, her face pale and drawn. Her voice was shaking. "I'm sorry I struck you but there was no excuse for what you did. Insulting my friends."

I looked at Chloris. She didn't have an answer ready yet.

"Futhermore," Mom said angrily, "as long as you're my daughter and live under my roof you will listen to me and obey me." Before Chloris had a chance to answer that, Mom added in a softer tone, "I admit I was wrong to insist that my good time come before yours. I'm sorry I wasn't fair about it. But I never knew you were planning to go away on this same weekend. You should have told me about it earlier. This way it all happened so fast, I couldn't think straight. So I'm sorry, too." Her hand reached out again. "Maybe next time we'll work it out better."

Chloris didn't weaken again. "I meant to tell you," she yelled. "I was going to, but I never got the chance."

Mom was shaking her head sadly. "You still have to ask my permission," she said. "I can't have you going off with just anybody."

Chloris slammed her napkin down. "I don't go

out with just *anybody*. I go out with my friends. All my friends were going. So why couldn't I?"

Mom looked at her, exasperated now. She went to the range and refilled her coffee cup. "We still never discussed it, did we? If it wasn't for Jennifer, I wouldn't have known where you were going or whom you were going with."

Chloris looked at me, angrily, the old familiar gleam in her eyes. "Thanks a lot," she said.

"Big deal." I got up and took my glass and plate to the sink and began washing them off.

"You can leave them, Jenny," Mom said. "I'll do them later."

I kept on washing them. Now I was angry myself. "Big deal," I said. "Its no big deal."

Chloris brought her dishes and glass over. "Here. You can do mine, too, while you're at it."

I rinsed mine off and put them on the drainboard. "Yeah, sure," I said. I dropped the dish rag on her plate. "Maybe on your birthday. Remind me."

Chloris said, "Thanks a lot." She dropped her dishes in the sink. "Anyway, Mom said she would do them."

"Big deal," I said again. I wondered how many more times I was going to say that. "Thanks for the eggs," I said to Mom. "I'm going to bed."

"Me, too," Chloris said. "Leave the light on."

"I can't hear you," I said. "Suddenly I got deaf. Also, if you want my opinion, you're pretty dumb."

Chloris looked at me, annoyed. "Oh, yeah?"

"Yeah," I said. "You forgot your new coat."

Chloris stared.

Mom was smiling, looking interested. "Oh? Did you get a new coat?"

Chloris sighed. "Yeah. For the trip up there."

"Maybe next time," Mom said cheerfully. "The snow won't go way. Can I see it on you?"

Chloris shrugged. "Okay, I'll get it," she said reluctantly.

As I went out, I said over my shoulder, "She looks terrific in it. Miss Pepperoni Pizza Queen of the year."

Then I walked airily out of the room, feeling better about everything. I got undressed again, got into bed, and put out the light.

I left the bedroom door open this time. I didn't hear any more angry voices from Chloris or Mom. It was the end of the incident for now, I felt. Mom had made her point about Chloris not going away without permission, and admitted she was wrong in putting her own happiness first, not being fair about their weekend plans.

Mom was still too anxious to have a happy home and wouldn't risk another argument at this time over her future plans with dating men. No more than she was the type who would ask Chloris' permission about whom to date. Next time there would probably be another big scene, but for now this one seemed to have ended peacefully. I could hear them talking softly. I felt better about that and fell asleep.

Some time later, I felt somebody shaking me. It was Chloris. She was sitting on the edge of my bed. "Where's Mom?" I said.

"She went to sleep."

"Good idea," I said. "I was sleeping, too." I closed my eyes and turned away from her.

Chloris laughed. "You're weird. I know you're dying to hear all about my trip."

"What trip? You didn't get to go anyplace."

"That's what you think."

I turned around and looked at her. "Well, hurry it up. I'm sleepy."

She laughed again, a bubbling laugh deep in her throat. "Well, for one thing, Wayne and I didn't hit it off at all. That pepperoni-pizza freak. I said he was weird, didn't I?"

"Yeah," I said. "So why did you go with him?"

She shrugged. "Anyway it was a no-no from the start. I guess all that pepperoni every night can warp your brain."

I sat up, interested now. "How come?"

Chloris grimaced. "I don't know how he got the idea, but he had the notion he and I were going to sleep together up there."

"He did? How could you tell?"

She made another wry face. "He kept talking about it. About how great it was going to be. Just him and me all alone together in that lodge up there. Making out, he said. Like I always wanted to with him, he said. Can you imagine that kind of freaky weirdo? All I wanted to do was to go up to Mammoth to go skiing with the kids, not to sleep with this pepperoni-pizza freak."

I was wide awake now. My clock said five o'clock. In a little while it would be morning. "So how did you get out of it?"

Chloris smiled. She pushed her hair back. "We had to stop some place for gas. Out of town some place. Antelope Valley. Near Palmdale, I think. So I got out of the car. Said I was going to the rest room. Only I kept going instead. Around the other side. And I flagged down a car and got a ride home."

I looked at her. "So what took you so long?"

Chloris sighed. "That was the first ride. This fellow was going to Palm Springs. He wanted to take me with him."

"How old was he?"

Chloris laughed and clapped her hands together. "About forty or fifty. But I didn't want to go to Palm Springs. So he set me down some place. The next driver was a lady. She got lost on the freeway and took me to Pasadena."

"Gy! Then what happened?"

"She got mad because she got off at the wrong ramp. Then she remembered she had a sister in Pasadena and decided to stay there instead. She told me she was very sorry to inconvenience me. I told Mom all about it."

"What did Mom say?"

Chloris shrugged. "She told me I was an irresponsible person. And that I spoiled her weekend."

"And what did you say?"

Chloris smiled. "I said I was sorry again."

I stared at her. "Only you're really not, right?"

"Why should I care about her weekend? Look what happened to mine. I could have been skiing!"

"You never would have made it even if you hadn't ducked out of Wayne's car," I said. "There's a big blizzard coming there. At Mammoth and June Lake. It was on the TV news."

"Really?"

I nodded. "You'll see in tomorrow's paper."

Chloris laughed softly. "Poor Wayne. I hope he's not too cold."

"What about Sue Brook and your other friends? Don't you care what happens to them?"

Choris shrugged. "Well, it was their idea to begin with. I only went along for the ride. They'll be okay."

"All you care about is yourself," I said.

Chloris nodded several times. "You're darn right."

"That's all you ever care about. Just yourself."

Chloris looked surprised. "Well, what else is there?"

"You don't care that Mom and I were worried sick."

She shrugged. "I never told you to worry. That was your own trip."

I looked at her. She didn't get what I was trying to say. No more than I understood her.

I turned around and lay down again, pulling the blanket around me. "I was going to say I was sorry I hit you and cut your lip. I don't think I'm sorry anymore."

Chloris laughed. "It's okay. I would have hit you, too."

"You mean if I went away for a weekend?"

"Especially if you went with a weirdo," Chloris said.

38

Harold the Hawk bobbed his head. "It's understandable," he said. "I can understand your doing it."

"You can?"

"Absolutely. I'm sure I would have done the same myself."

We were in the bus. On our way to the Saturday night movie. My second date with Harold the Hawk. He looked all dressed up and clean. Not a bandage on him, not even a little Band-aid.

"But I hit her hard. Practically all my might. I might have hurt her."

"Well, you didn't, apparently. Only cut her lip, you said."

"I was so mad. I really flipped out that time, Harold."

He nodded. "It's love-hate, that's all it was, Jenny. Perfectly natural. You love your sister so much, and she worried you so by doing what she did, you nearly went crazy with fear. So when you saw her, it all came out, all the love and all the hate for making you so dependent on her."

The bus stopped. Harold got up and helped me off. He even put a hand on my arm to help me get down the bus steps.

"The movie's that way," he said.

"Are we on time?"

He checked his watch. "Perfect timing. We got seven minutes to cross Wilshire and get on that line."

"How about later? Will we have time for something to eat?"

"Well, there's a ten twenty-two bus which gets us back fifteen minutes early, and a ten forty-five bus which gets us back twelve minutes late. I mean, if you have to check in at eleven."

I grabbed his arm. "After Mom waited until nearly five in the morning for Chloris to come home, she's not gonna get too steamed if I'm not home by eleven exactly."

He shrugged and yanked me across the street past the last car in our way. "Right on. Hey, will you look at that line. It's nearly around the block."

"That's okay, Harold," I said. "I don't mind. It only proves it must be a good movie."

"I hope you're right. Otherwise I'm blowing seven bucks."

I waved my purse. "We can go Dutch if you want."

Harold wagged his head negative. "No, thanks. I've got to get used to spending money on you, Jen."

"You do?" I said. "Why?"

"Well," he said.

We got on line and suddenly I noticed that Harold and I were still holding hands.

"You were going to tell me why, Harold."

"Oh, yeah. How about that." He looked around. "Hey, this is really a long line."

I waited.

Harold cleared his throat. "Well, you're very dependable, for one thing. I mean you're always on time. I come to the door and you're right there. All ready and everything."

Harold stopped talking and we both waited.

"Any other reason?" I said.

"You're more dependable than my skateboard, I'll tell you that. Darn thing is always breaking. Costing me a ton of money."

"But you told me your skateboard is your very best friend, Harold. Remember?"

"Well, yeah. I know." He looked down at our entwined hands. He lifted his hand along with mine and swung them. "You know, everybody is talking about teenagers shooting up dope and getting pregnant, and here we are and all we're doing is holding hands on a long line waiting to get into some movie."

"I guess we must be weird, Harold."

He thought about it. "Yeah. How about that."

The line began to move faster and we got in and found two seats on the side. They weren't the greatest seats but I didn't care. The movie was okay. Harold the Hawk put his arm over the back of my seat and held it there longer this time before it fell asleep on him. He tried it a few more times before giving up.

"I guess I got to get used to movies," he said.

We had chili after the movie and milkshakes. Harold got rid of some more money. We made the later bus home.

"Do you think we ought to try kissing good night or something?" Harold said.

"Are you sure you can't do this with your skateboard?" I said.

We kissed and after a while we stopped. Harold looked at his watch. "Hey, seven seconds! That's not bad first time, is it?"

"Good night, Harold," I said. "Thanks for the movie and everything."

He stood there, nodding, checking his watch.

"Yeah, how about that. I bet we can do ten next time, if we try."

"You're weird, Harold," I said.

"Hey, you going to school Monday?"

"Sure. Why?"

"Hey, yeah. That's right. How about that. I'll see you then, huh?"

"I hope so, Harold. Good night."

He waved and walked away backward.

"Harold, look out for those steps."

He got up quickly. "It's okay. I should have remembered that. Six steps here. Eleven steps at the first level."

He waved again and ran off. I had a feeling he was going to jump the last eleven steps and didn't want to look.

But I did, anyway.

He cleared them all, didn't fall and didn't break his leg. I was glad I looked. It really was a remarkable jump. When he ran off, he was just barely limping.

When I got inside, Mom was watching TV. "Did you have a good time?"

"Terrific," I said. "Sensational."

"Chloris is asleep," she said. "She's exhausted."

"Sorry if I'm late," I said.

"It's all right. As long as you had fun."

"Seven seconds," I said.

"What?" Mom said.

"Yeah, how about that," I said.

Mom looked at me. "Are you all right?"

"Marvelous," I said.

When I was brushing my teeth before going to bed, I looked at my lips just as Chloris had studied hers. Harold, I said to myself, you're so right. I bet we do ten next time easy.

Weird how people change, isn't it?

ABOUT THE AUTHOR

KIN PLATT was the noted newspaper caricaturist and cartoonist of the popular comic strip "Mr. and Mrs." for the *New York Herald Tribune* before turning to books. His outstanding and controversial young adult novels include *Chloris and the Creeps, Chloris and the Freaks, Sinbad and Me, Hey Dummy, Mystery of the Witch Who Wouldn't, Headman, The Doomsday Gang* and *The Boy Who Could Make Himself Disappear* (which was made into the film, *Baxter*.) His adult mysteries feature the Los Angeles private eye Max Roper, whose latest adventures are found in *The Screwball King Murder*. *Headman* was one of the 1975 ALA Best Books for Young Adults and *Sinbad and Me* won a Mystery Writers Award. Mr. Platt lives in Los Angeles.

TEENAGERS FACE LIFE AND LOVE

Choose books filled with fun and adventure, discovery and disenchantment, failure and conquest, triumph and tragedy, life and love.

☐	13359	**THE LATE GREAT ME** Sandra Scoppettone	$1.95
☐	13691	**HOME BEFORE DARK** Sue Ellen Bridgers	$1.75
☐	12501	**PARDON ME, YOU'RE STEPPING ON MY EYEBALL!-** Paul Zindel	$1.95
☐	11091	**A HOUSE FOR JONNIE O.** Blossom Elfman	$1.95
☐	12025	**ONE FAT SUMMER** Robert Lipsyte	$1.75
☐	13184	**I KNOW WHY THE CAGED BIRD SINGS** Maya Angelou	$2.25
☐	13013	**ROLL OF THUNDER, HEAR MY CRY** Mildred Taylor	$1.95
☐	12741	**MY DARLING, MY HAMBURGER** Paul Zindel	$1.95
☐	12420	**THE BELL JAR** Sylvia Plath	$2.50
☐	13897	**WHERE THE RED FERN GROWS** Wilson Rawls	$2.25
☐	11829	**CONFESSIONS OF A TEENAGE BABOON** Paul Zindel	$1.95
☐	11838	**OUT OF LOVE** Hilma Wolitzer	$1.50
☐	13352	**SOMETHING FOR JOEY** Richard E. Peck	$1.95
☐	13440	**SUMMER OF MY GERMAN SOLDIER** Bette Greene	$1.95
☐	13693	**WINNING** Robin Brancato	$1.95
☐	13628	**IT'S NOT THE END OF THE WORLD** Judy Blume	$1.95

Buy them at your local bookstore or use this handy coupon for ordering: